The Lark and the Laurel

Barbara Willard

Drawings by Gareth Floyd

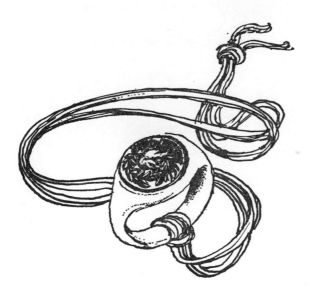

Longman Young Books

LONGMAN GROUP LIMITED
LONDON

First published 1970

SBN 582 15852 4

For Grace, with love and gratitude

Set in 12pt Imprint, 1 pt. leaded
Printed in Great Britain
by Ebenezer Baylis and Son Ltd
The Trinity Press, Worcester, and London

The Lark and the Laurel

Contents

32 lines from Medieval Latin Lyrics tr. Helen Waddell reproduced on pp. 105–106 by permission of Constable, London.

1
To Mantlemass

Cecily had been brought to Mantlemass at dusk. Already bitterly fatigued by the long ride from London, by the haste and surprise and fear of it all, she had clung to her father as if she were drowning and only he of all the world could save her. Her own misery, loud and ugly, clamoured in her ears and she could not stop it in spite of the distaste and anger she saw in her father's face. She had never dared to behave to him in such a way before. She heard him say, 'She is distraught, sister,' and he dragged her hands from their stranglehold and thrust her roughly into the arms of her aunt. Cecily struggled, but her aunt held her firmly, repeating over and over again words that were meant to soothe. Two of the maids joined in, and the old nurse they called Goody Ann, until the hall seemed full of struggling, protesting people, their shadows bobbing in the light of torches held against the growing dark by her aunt's men servants. Giles and Humfrey were there, too, to increase the crowd—her father's men who would ride away with him to the coast and so across the sea to France. When they went there would be no one left with Cecily whom she had ever known.

Getting the girl to bed had been like fighting with a mad creature. She was past all reason and it was almost a relief when her aunt struck her such a blow across the face that she was shocked into silence. She heard her aunt say in a commanding voice, 'Drink, now—drink this!' She had swallowed the draught before she knew what she she was doing. 'Now she will sleep,' someone said. And she did sleep, instantly, falling into a black pit where she was shut away even from her own misery. . . .

When Cecily woke the night was over. Without opening her eyes she called, as she always did call, 'Alys! Alys! I am awake.' And always when she called Alys leapt up from her bed across the doorway, though it were midnight or the smallest hour before sunrise, to ask what she needed. Only this morning, for the first time ever, there was no Alys to answer Cecily's call. For the first time ever, Cecily was in a room alone, with none to attend her, none to care whether she slept or woke.

Although the bed curtains were closed she could see light through a crack towards the foot of the bed. Beyond the curtains, beyond the strange house, the sun was shining. It was the last week in August, as bright with hope and promise as with sunshine for the long war was over that had torn England into factions. A new king had been crowned on the battlefield beside the gashed and naked body of the old—a new king who would stand neither for York nor Lancaster but a union of both—a

Tudor king. He would not forget his faithful followers, supporters of the Lancastrian cause. For them—a happy ending to the years of strife renewed and renewed again until this final triumph. For the others? Well, a loyal Yorkist would be recognised, no doubt, for that loyalty, even though it was to a lost cause. But there were others, mindful of their own advantage, who had changed their coats and now must expect the fate of traitors. At best, for them, the exile into which Cecily's own father had ridden after leaving her in her aunt's keeping.

All this Cecily had learnt yesterday, which seemed now part of another, vanished world. She had been standing down at the waterside on the stone steps where the barge was moored. Alys was with her, as always, and they were feeding crusts to the swans that rocked gently against the river's tide. Cecily knew that, fifty paces away, her father was walking on the terrace before the house, and she knew without being told that something untoward had happened or must happen soon. She did not turn to look at him, for she was always very frightened of him, but the sensation of urgency about the place made her palms sweat and her scalp prickle.

'There is no more bread, Alys.'

Alys looked about her, but there was no servant at hand.

'Fetch it yourself,' said Cecily, a little sharply.

Alys hesitated, glancing from Cecily towards her father. She was a constant attendant—night or day she was at Cecily's side and seemed to exist only to serve. Or perhaps to guard. This thought had once or twice found its way into Cecily's mind. She repeated her order, now, and Alys went quickly towards the house.

There was very little traffic on the river. Only one barge went by, and that was in midstream. Cecily turned away automatically, for she was alone and must not notice strangers. So she was facing the house when the visitor arrived. It was her uncle Digby, her dead mother's brother, who seldom came to the house in Blackfriars. He strode out unannounced on to the terrace where her father was pacing. His face and beard were as dusty as his boots, so it was plain that he had ridden hard through the dry summer day.

In the very instant of their meeting, the voices of the two men rose harshly, and the sensation of alarm increased a hundredfold. Cecily swung back to the swans, as though in a dutiful attempt not to hear what was being said. But the birds, ruffled by her neglect, sailed relentlessly away while the words of the two men, violent and clear, forced her attention.

'They pulled the crown out from under the bushes,' the newcomer cried. 'It had rolled there through the blood and the dust. They set it, dripping, on Richmond's head—I have it from a witness—and all there cried out *God Save the King* and *Amen*—and they raised his standard for the soldiers to see. So died the old order, Sir Thomas. So begins the new. You will know better than I what this can mean.'

'To some,' replied Sir Thomas Jolland.

'To you,' Cecily heard her uncle say. 'And to yours. Why else am I here—at some risk to myself?'

'I thank you for it.'

'I am concerned for my dead sister's child, not for her father.'

Sir Thomas called, 'Cecily! Come here to me.' She picked up her skirts and came as fast as manners allowed. 'Go indoors,' he said. 'Call Alys to get you ready for travelling.' She stood trembling, her eyes on the ground at his feet. 'At once!' he cried.

Her uncle broke in. 'I will see to the girl. Leave her to me and get on your way, brother-in-law. Better for all of us when you are gone. I would give your girl shelter myself, in spite of everything. But you know well that my wife is kin to the Tudors. It is not wise. Still, on my honour I will see your daughter safe, Sir Thomas.'

'Cecily, do as I bid you—go indoors,' her father repeated. As she went she heard him say angrily, 'This is my treasure. If I may not spend it, at least I will see it safely put away.'

The sun shone on Cecily's neck as she stumbled into the house. She was half sick with fright. What did *safely put away* mean? Once, last spring, she had run singing through the orchard with her head bare and her hair streaming on her shoulders—and her father had seen her and caught her. He had threatened as he struck her repeatedly to put her into a convent—his younger sister was abbess of a foundation near York. If Cecily could not be modest by taste and inclination, he had told her, then the habit of modesty must be forced upon her. *Safely put away* sounded the same alarm in the girl's mind as she had experienced then . . . Or perhaps she was to die, and that was to be her safety—then she would pay finally for the sin of being a useless daughter instead of a stalwart son. Her old nurse, long since sent away, had promised her that when she died she would see her mother again, but her mother was a forgotten stranger, faceless and voiceless.

As she went into the house, Cecily was calling shrilly for Alys, fear pinching her throat so cruelly that she found breathing difficult.

Alys came running, looking excited and strange.

'I went to the kitchens for bread . . . Lord Digby's men are there . . . Oh lady! The tales they tell! The terror of it all!'

'Is the world ending?'

'There is a new king. King Richard is dead on the

battlefield. His followers must surely all disperse and fly to safety! Henry Tudor is our king!'

'The Earl of Richmond. I heard my uncle say so . . . We are to travel, Alys.'

Cecily understood her father's plight very well. A Lancastrian by birth and service, Sir Thomas Jolland had changed his allegiance when it seemed expedient to become a Yorkist and King Richard's man. Better for him if he had supported the House of York from the start of the quarrels—loyalty to the losing side was more admirable to a victor than the shift and grab of an opportunist. Cecily knew little enough of the world, but at least she knew that when men invited the name of *traitor* they must watch out for their heads. So must her father now.

Alys was wailing, 'How will you do without me? Who will care for you?'

'Why—what do you mean by that?' cried Cecily.

Alys had long grey eyes and she put her hand over them as she answered. 'Sir Thomas called to me as I crossed the hall. You must go one way, lady, and I am to go another.'

This news stunned Cecily. She had never been alone in all her life. First there had been nurses to care for her, then Alys had been given to her for her own. How indeed was Cecily to manage without her? She had never brushed her own hair, or knotted a girdle . . . The image of her aunt, the abbess, loomed uncomfortably.

'Where am I to go?'

'To Mantlemass, lady.'

'*There*?' It was not the convent, certainly, but the household of her father's elder sister, Elizabeth Fitz-Edmund. Time and time again Dame Elizabeth had asked for Cecily's company—the girl motherless, Dame Elizabeth a widow made the suggestion a very suitable one.

But Sir Thomas's reply had always been brutally to the point. Twice when her aunt had come to London and visited the house, Cecily had been locked away. She had heard a strong, unfamiliar voice ringing across the great hall, 'One day, brother, I promise you I shall release your prisoner.' Cecily's lip had curled at the expression, for Alys had long ago convinced her of the reason for being kept so close. It was because, Alys said, her father had in mind a high and mighty husband for her; one so noble he would demand for his bride a lily untouched by any contact with the base ways of the world.

It suited Cecily to accept this flattery, but in her heart she retained a doubt she would never have spoken aloud, even to Alys. She had known for some years that men sold their daughters to advantage themselves, though they called it *giving in marriage*. Her nurse had told her of a little cousin on her mother's side, a Digby heiress, who was contracted in her cradle to the eldest son of a powerful father. By this marriage estates would be enlarged and titles come by. The boy died of a fever in childhood, but the interest of the two fathers was not to be set aside. So the second son took his dead brother's place as the promised husband. He, too, died in his turn before he reached even twelve years old, and it was the third son who finally gained the bride. A daughter was an easy enough price to pay in such a bargain between parents.

This story had never been forgotten, and Cecily thought of it now, when her father so lightly consigned her to the sister he spoke of as harsh and headstrong and unwomanly.

'Where is Mantlemass, lady?' Alys was asking. 'I have never heard.'

'I think it is south from London . . .' began Cecily. Then she paused, *knowing* it was south from London, and therefore well on the way to the coast where her father would find a boat to take him into France. For this reason and no other, for his own convenience, he would leave her there, shedding her as thankfully as he would some cumbersome baggage. If his younger sister's convent had stood where Mantlemass stood, then he would have left her at the convent. Realising this, Cecily flew into a fury and stamped and struck out at Alys, catching her hard on the right ear. 'Fetch my blue gown! Make me a bundle for my goods. I'll have the pearl my uncle gave me for my christening and the cross with rubies that was my mother's. Do as I bid you! Hurry, girl!'

Alys bit her lip as she clutched her burning ear, and her eyes were full of tears. An hour, half an hour ago, Cecily would have accepted the tears as grief at the parting. Now she wondered, for treachery seemed in the air.

It was a little after noon when they rode out of London, Sir Thomas in a plain, untrimmed cloak and dun-colour hose, his cap low on his brow. His two men, Giles and Humfrey, were muffled, too, while Cecily was veiled as closely as any princess. The day was fine, the world about its business. Part of that business gathered knots of men and women at house doors and crossways—as the subjects of a new king, they had plenty to discuss and surmise. But when London and its neighbouring villages were left behind and they came to deeper country, cattle and pigs and the harvest seemed to leave little time for gossiping.

They rode steadily, since a speeding rider is more to be remembered. Once the sun began to decline a little they increased their pace. The open roads gave way to country tracks with dusty hedgerows. The horses' hoofs thudded here, giving an impression of urgency that the journey had lacked till now. Cecily awoke out of a numb misery into an active despair. She was to be abandoned among strangers. There would be no single face at Mantlemass

that she had ever seen before. Tears filled her eyes and
poured down her cheeks and she tried to dry them on her
veil. She rode along crying bitterly, sniffing and gulping
like a child of half her age, wishing she might have been
riding pillion behind her father, so that she could speak
to him and try to wheedle him.

The man Giles was riding behind Cecily and he moved
up close and spoke gently to her. 'Hush,' he said. 'Hush,
my dear lady. You will make yourself ill.'

'Get back to your place,' she snapped, her face ugly
with misery. She spurred forward in her turn till she
was riding at her father's elbow. 'Let me come with you,
sir.'

'Impossible.'

'I would not be a burden.'

'Yes,' he said, 'you would be a burden. A man in flight
needs both hands free.'

'Oh please—oh father, I beg you . . . I shall be alone . . .
I shall be alone . . .'

'You must stay till I send for you.'

'When . . . ?'

'Can I tell when? Be sensible.'

Hysteria made her shrill. 'I shall die! I shall pine and
die. . . .'

'Is it my choice?' he cried angrily. 'It is God's will
that we have a new king—but for me it had as well be
Satan's . . . Oh stop your wailing! Where's your pride,
girl?'

It was impossible for Cecily to check her tears. She rode
at her father's side, sobbing and biting her lips. Her face
was blotched and swollen.

Presently they mounted rising ground and looked out
over a vast expanse that was half forest and half heath.
The sun was setting and the atmosphere, a little hazy,
seemed as flushed as the sky itself. At a distance some

light could be seen, and Cecily thought perhaps men had lit beacons to honour the new king. But Sir Thomas said there was iron smelting in these parts and the glow came from furnaces.

They were almost at Mantlemass and the parting of their ways.

That sunset had promised a fine morning, and fine it was. Cecily stirred in her bed at last and sat up. Her head swam. She pushed back the covers and pulled the curtains, looking out into the room like a mouse from a hole, not quite able to believe that there was no one there to watch for her waking. Now the sun had shifted and was plunging a long blade of light through the greenish glass of the deep-set window. Cecily got out of bed slowly and carefully. The wood floor was bare but rubbed to a high polish with beeswax. There was a vast press against the far wall, a chest along the foot of the bed, two stools and a heavy, rough-looking table. She looked around her with deep curiosity, then moved to the window. She stood peering through the window panes, unable to see more than confused treetops and a sky apparently clear of cloud. Then she found a pane that opened when she pushed it. The clean morning air gushed in at her, blowing full from the south and carrying still, more than twenty miles inland, some memory of the sea. The coolness on her forehead stopped the ache and she stood there at the window until she thought guiltily what Alys would say to her if she were there. She shut the window quickly— then opened it again at once. The gesture strangely elated her. She was unaccustomed to opening windows but there was no one to prevent her doing so if she wished. She was alone, she was deserted—she was very much afraid—yet she knew for the first time that she existed in her own right. She was herself. She could call her soul her own. A conscious resistance to her new circumstances hardened unexpectedly as she recognised this.

Her clothes were lying tidily over the chest and she moved towards them, rather warily. The skirt of her blue gown was dusty from yesterday's ride and she brushed it with her hand, ineffectually and with great distaste. Then she shook out the gown more vigorously and looked uneasily at the fastenings. First, however, she must deal with her linen petticoat, and she struggled into it modestly under the folds of her bedgown. She fought with the folds of both garments and emerged triumphantly—she had contrived to tie the petticoat points though they might prove more difficult to undo.

She was half into the blue gown when she heard foot-steps outside her door. The key turned in the lock, and she knew for the first time that she had been held captive.

The door opened and her aunt came into the room.

Cecily was at a great disadvantage—half dressed, her hair hanging unbrushed about her shoulders, no shoes on her feet. Holding the dress up and pushing back her hair, which was straight and fine, and as fair, she had been told, as her mother's, she contrived the necessary courtesy to her aunt.

'God bless you this fine morning, niece.'

'And you, madam,' murmured Cecily.

'I see you have slept well and are now composed.' Her voice was brisk and she looked herself as though she had been nothing but composed for many years—though the effect was of strength rather than tranquillity. She was tall, dark-browed under her widow's cap, straight-backed, steady-eyed. Her mouth was firmer than a woman's mouth is usually allowed to be. A dark, roughish gown without any adornment made her appear more like a farmer's wife than the widow of a gentleman. Her hands were without any ring but her marriage band, and they

2

were brown from the summer weather. She wore leather shoes with hard, thick soles, such as Cecily had never seen before. While she eyed her aunt nervously, taking in all this, so Dame ⎸Elizabeth FitzEdmund eyed her niece, in a steady, summing-up fashion that made Cecily start to tremble. 'Now, child, you must stay calm,' her aunt said. 'You need not fear for your father. Sir Thomas was always a good manager.' There was a sharp note in her voice that suggested a sister could feel less than love for a brother.

'He will go into France,' Cecily managed.

'For sure. He has friends there from other days.'

'I think he was at the French court once,' Cecily said, her voice so small and faint it was barely audible.

'Come to the window and let me see what manner of girl you are,' her aunt said, taking her by the wrist. 'You are still trembling, Cecily Jolland. Why? It is not for you to endure your father's misfortunes.' All this time she had not smiled, but now a flicker broke up the firmness of her expression. 'I will tell you this at once—I, too, have been alone and forced to make a new life. I, too, had your father to thank for it. For me, there was great tribulation. For you—it shall be simpler.'

'Shall it, madam?'

'Trust me—and I will see you happy. Believe me. Have faith in me. Obey me. All shall be well.'

Cecily's hand moved in her aunt's grasp. She said faintly—'Yes, madam.'

'Trust me, I said. And that means—do not struggle.' Her aunt smiled at last, though wryly, and patted Cecily's hand. 'How old are you?'

'I am sixteen years old in the New Year.'

'And eleven of those years without a mother. Well, you must be my daughter now. But let us understand one another. I have only this one purpose for you: to give back what has been taken away.'

'Alys?' asked Cecily hopefully. Then corrected herself, 'My father?'

'Not your father—and not that girl I saw at Black-friars—that girl with the sly eyes. She's plans of her own, I'd say.'

Cecily had opened her mouth to protest at *sly eyes*, but she closed it again remembering her own sudden doubts of Alys yesterday.

'What plans?' she asked.

'How should I know? There's no need to bother with your Alys now.' Dame Elizabeth put Cecily's hand from her, then, as though she had done with it for the time being. 'It is almost dinner time—you slept so late. I shall send Meg to help you today. But you must learn to look after yourself. We are not in the world of fashion here.' She twitched at the bed curtain in passing. 'There's a rent in the damask; Meg shall mend it . . . And, Cecily— pray remember that God gave you a voice to speak out with, not to coddle underneath your breath.'

She went out of the room, closing the door behind her. But the key did not turn.

2
Her Father's Daughter

After her aunt had gone, Cecily stayed a long time without moving. The strangeness of her state was almost overwhelming. Dame Elizabeth had called her a prisoner when she was at home, but what was she now? There was no escape from Mantlemass. If her father had been a gaoler, what was her aunt? What, indeed, was her aunt? A woman unlike any other Cecily had heard of. At her husband's death she had instantly left his house by the river Thames at Sheen, near the royal palace, and come to this lonely place to make a new life, one unsupported by any but her own courage and determination. About this new gaoler, then, if that was what she was to be called, Cecily felt deep curiosity.

She thought of her father and of how he, too, must make a new life. It was true that he had friends in France —once, in fact, she had been with him there herself. It was there that her mother had died of the sickness that struck them both. When the young Cecily recovered from this illness she could not even recall her mother's face. It was only in a curious, feverish dream that she believed she was able, even now, to recognise her voice. In this strange experience that came to her sometimes between sleep and waking, or when she had some chill or infection upon her, she saw first the smile of a dark-bearded man with a jewel in his ear; then a nodding sombre greybeard in a purple gown. Soon came a jumble of voices, the laughter of men and women crowding in a small chamber. Next there was a boy somewhere near her own age—she must still have been very young since her mother was certainly there—a boy who advanced and greeted her, kissing her between the eyes as gently and quickly as some small shy animal that licks an offered hand then frisks away . . . At this point the picture always began to fade, and as she lost it she seemed to hear her mother saying *My bird—my pretty bird* . . . Although she knew that it was she, the child Cecily, who was her mother's pretty bird, she always struggled to see clearly the device of a bird flying, carrying something in its beak. It could be a dove with a branch of olive—or a raven bearing a flower whose berries would be poison. . . .

They were ringing a bell somewhere below in the big house. That surely meant dinner time and Cecily began in a flustered way to pull her gown into place, dismayed by the fastenings and ready to cry at her own helplessness. Before that happened, one of the maids came running to help and then showed her the way to the hall.

Sir Thomas Jolland, it had been said, kept a state beyond his means and rank. But here at Mantlemass the whole way of life was different. The house was no more than ten or fifteen years old, a manor farm, a yeoman's dwelling of a kind increasingly to be found in the countryside. It was one of several such properties inherited by Dame Elizabeth from her husband. She held it from the Crown, and with it certain privileges—the right to keep hawk and hound for the taking of venison and game, and to collect settled tithes from the tenantry.

'Come to table, niece,' Dame Elizabeth said, turning from the knot of men she was talking to by the door. At this they bowed and left her. 'Those are my fellow traders,' she said. 'You must understand that I am a trader now. And there is no call for any man or woman to smile at that. In fact I see you have more horror than humour in your expression.'

'It pleases you to be sharp with me . . .' Cecily mumbled, at a loss to understand what her aunt was talking about.

'Well, it is all true as daylight and brings me pride, pleasure—and profit. I shall show you my trade presently. Now—come to your dinner.'

Dame Elizabeth swept on into the hall, but Cecily hesitated on the threshold. The place seemed full of people and noisy with such boisterous talk as she had never heard before. When Sir Thomas entered his own hall, all fell silent and stood to do him a courtesy. But as Dame Elizabeth moved to her place, she merely added to the noise—shouting out to a man standing halfway down the table—leaning across to say something to a woman on the far side of the board, and breaking into laughter at her reply. It was only when the mistress of the house stood at the head of her own table that the household servants who would share the meal fell silent.

Cecily still hung back. The hall was a quarter of the size of her father's, with one long table and only two sideboards for serving. At one end was an enormous hearth with a canopied flue. It was not the mean size of the hall, however, or its heating arrangements, that made Cecily hang back.

'Here is your place, niece,' her aunt called—and immediately twelve or fourteen heads were turned in the direction of the newcomer. 'Come now, Cecily—these are my people and they shall be yours. You need not hide your face.' She smiled at the girl, kindly enough, as she sat down nervously. 'You will not have seen such a house as this, I daresay. I shall show you how it has many rooms, small and convenient. A great man's hall is as bustling as a market place. But we lesser folk are growing more private.'

'So many windows,' Cecily managed, in her small voice. 'I have hardly seen so much glass, madam.' She had hardly seen so many fellow diners, for that matter, for either she and Alys were served food upstairs in the

solar, or else there was none but her father at table with
her.

'The glass comes from the west of this country,' Dame
Elizabeth said. 'In summer the ways are hard and dry
and I have ridden into those parts and seen the glass come
liquid from the furnaces. A prettier sight than the iron
worked by my own tenants hereabouts.'

'Glass may be broken by intruders,' Cecily offered,
primly quoting what she had heard her father say.

'Perhaps—where intruders are to be found. Here, we
are all too busy. We depend one upon the other, as you
will surely see. This is thought to be a wild part of the
countryside and many outlaws seek refuge here. Yet we
all serve and respect one another. The forest binds us,
one to the other.' She turned to Cecily and took the
girl's hand in her own, holding it palm uppermost. 'This
is the hand of a cosseted gentlewoman. What skills has
it?'

'It can embroider with silks.'

'And—?'

'I have—I had—my lute.'

'And—?'

Cecily was silent. She could think of nothing more a
gentle hand need do.

'Now take my hand,' said Dame Elizabeth. 'This hand,
also, is the hand of a gentlewoman. But it has taught itself
to grow strong. It has learnt many skills. This hand will
bake, will brew, will write accounts fairly, will strike in
anger, soothe in sickness, be silk or iron on a rein. It will
cull herbs, bind up sores, carve meat, shear a fleece or gut
a coney. Yes, indeed—you will tell me it has grown hard
with all this service. But I shall answer that it has grown
proud.'

'Yes, madam,' said Cecily, wondering if her aunt was at
least halfway to madness.

'And so, dear niece, shall yours.'

Cecily clasped her threatened hand with its fellow.
They were smooth hands, the fingers frail and pliable,
graceful and useless. Yet honesty told her they could
strike in anger as much as her aunt's hands might; and
even her father had praised her for the way she could
control her horse.

The rest of the company had all this time remained
standing down either side of the table. Now there came
hurrying to Dame Elizabeth's side a small thin man in a
shabby brown habit. Dame Elizabeth rose, and Cecily
with her, and the newcomer said a somewhat breathless
Grace. After the Amens, the maids began at once to serve
the dinner.

Cecily was hungry by now, but distress at her aunt's
talk, resentment at eating in this public fashion, closed
up her throat and the good food would not go down. Was
she to spend the rest of her life, then, in bondage to this
unwomanly woman with her plain clothes and her down-
right way of speech? Was it for this that her father had
kept her so carefully? *I have only one purpose*, her aunt
had told her, *to give back what has been taken away*. She
must have spoken whimsically—she could only have
meant these simple employments which any woman
might call her right, but which a lady carefully nurtured
would thankfully relinquish.

'She has come to be a daughter to me,' Dame Elizabeth
was saying to the friar. 'Cecily, Friar Paul is here from
time to time on his wanderings. He will hear our con-
fessions and say a mass for us . . . The child is sad at
losing her father,' she explained, 'but I shall see that she
is happy here as never in her life before.' She smiled
slightly. 'As you will see, she doubts this.'

'You are fortunate in a good guardian, my child,' said
Friar Paul. He was short of his front teeth and having

some trouble with his dinner. 'Give this good lady your daughterly duty and God will bless you both.'

Cecily made some murmured reply, and then the conversation went on without her. Her aunt and the friar spoke of country things, of harvest and next year's sowing, of pannage for hogs and the grazing of sheep. There were complaints of a neighbour who had felled a copse five years too young, and that led on to the urgent problem of wood being cut for charcoal to keep the furnaces and forges of that neighbourhood going summer and winter.

'We suffer too much from this,' Dame Elizabeth said. The roads are broken into bog by the carting of the iron. We shall soon be living in a quagmire. We shall have no timber, soon, to mend the barn roof or keep our fences against the deer.'

'But if men are given these materials in the earth and the skill to work them—there's a divine purpose that must be bowed to,' the friar answered.

'There's little divinity in the muck and the row of the forges,' Dame Elizabeth said coarsely. 'And if men stopped their quarrels there'd be no need of weapons.'

'So they would beat their swords into ploughshares,' replied Friar Paul, unexpectedly chuckling, 'and the noise would be just the same.'

'Well, it is a song I find hard on my ears, Friar Paul. I am concerned with quieter ways of trade. Unless they are clumsily killed, my coneys are as silent as shadows.'

None of this talk made the least sense to Cecily. Further down the table, the conversation was even less intelligible, for it was full of strange words. Across the table from the maids sat two or three men whose employment Cecily tried to guess. One looked very quiet and clerkly, though he wore secular dress, and another, broad-shouldered and bluff in manner, with a fine red beard, seemed to be laying down the law to any prepared to listen—or unable to avoid hearing. He might be her aunt's bailiff, Cecily thought, while the thin dark man listening with a half smile, was probably the manor reeve; he looked kindly, a good go-between for tenants and workers and dame of the manor alike.

'I come my way by Salehurst yesterd'y,' redbeard was saying, 'and I doddled by a bit where they make a goodish warren on stoachy ground—pilrag, maybe. That'll be Priory doing. Two of the monks come by Mantlemass last spring, and saw our warrens, and took the notion.'

'There's a slocksey way to talk of the brothers, Master Henty,' said the dark man, with a warning glance towards Friar Paul. 'What if the lady of the house hear what you say?'

'She does hear,' said Dame Elizabeth, snapping into the conversation so roughly that Cecily flinched. 'Mind your manners, Henty.'

'No offence, madam,' said Henty, but without humility.

'Then keep your opinions locked behind that fine great beard of yours—or there'll be offence in plenty and penalties to meet it.' She called to one of the maids, 'Serve me the sallet now, Bet. And a dish here for Friar Paul.' She glanced at Cecily. 'Drink your ale, niece. It will nourish you.'

Cecily drank obediently. The ale was strong and spicy and caught the back of her nose so sharply that she sneezed.

'God keep you,' said her aunt. Those who heard her, and had heard the sneeze, crossed themselves quickly, for all the world as though they thought the newcomer might have brought the plague from London.

'It was the ale tickled me. I am used to wine,' said Cecily sullenly. Talk broke out again and she sat silent, no longer even trying to make sense of what she heard. The voices had a roll to them and this allied to the outlandish words left her bewildered and bitterly lonely. Even her aunt spoke differently—there was little trace in her speech of the London English Cecily knew, and still less of the pinched accents in which Alys had so often mocked fashionable ladies she had heard, and which Cecily had often tried to imitate. These country people were worse than strangers—they were foreigners.

At last the meal ended, grace was said, Dame Elizabeth led the way from the table. Now, Cecily thought, she could be alone—she could run to her own room—she could bring the key to the other side of the lock and turn it firmly. . . .

Perhaps her aunt knew this, for she instantly cut off all retreat.

'Now, my child, I shall show you Mantlemass. If this is to be your home, then you must know it, walls and windows, barns and byres. Show me your feet . . . You shall be better shod once this dry spell is past—but today you can manage well enough. Pick up your skirts, or the hem will soon be soiled. We must get you more sensible wear than this fine stuff. Mary Butterwick and Meg shall set about it—Goody Ann's sight is not strong enough these days.' She looked rather sharply at Cecily, who had made no reply. 'What did I say about your voice? I cannot live with a silent niece.'

The change in her circumstances seemed brutally presented. Yet looking resentfully into her aunt's face, Cecily could find no cruelty in Dame Elizabeth's expression. She might have seen courage, boldness, honesty—and even loneliness, though certainly she could not have named it. Groping for reassurance, Cecily knew positively that though her aunt might have a high anger, though she might prove an opponent, she could not frighten. With this conviction there came a quick faint lifting of Cecily's spirit, so slight it was barely perceptible—yet like a crumb to a starving man suggesting most certainly that there was still bread in the world. . . .

Dame Elizabeth was proud of her new-fashioned manor house—she led the way to the winter parlour, quite apart from the hall, where she said they would dine in winter away from the draughts. Soon they came to the kitchen, where a woman was scouring pots with a girl and two kitchen boys to help her. Kitchen, bakehouse and brewery formed three sides of an inner court, and in its centre was the well. The cellars ran alongside and below the hall, well stocked with vats and butts. It was cold down there. In the corners the floor ran with water that trickled greenly in the rushlight Dame Elizabeth carried. It seemed like a place to hide away an enemy from the light of day, to hide him till he was forgotten, all but his bones. Cecily was glad to go up the stairs again, and then up once more to the bed chambers. Over these was a great loft reaching into the roof rafters.

'This is where the maids sleep,' Dame Elizabeth explained. 'Look how the chimney comes up from below. Put your hand on the wall here—it is warm. They are pampered, I can tell you.'

The high roof of the hall divided the house into two parts, and they had to descend and cross the hall, then mount another stairway to the solar. Here the furnishings were very handsome indeed. There were tapestries on the walls, and on the floor, too, in place of rushes. There was a fine carved dower chest, two enormous high-backed chairs, and many sconces to hold lights once dusk came down. And propped on a carved stand was an open book with letters picked out in gold, and designs of fruit and flowers, birds and animals in the wide margins.

'All these things were in my husband's house by the river. It was too prodigal to leave them—though I would have done so if it made any sense.' Dame Elizabeth's voice was non-committal, but the words painted a comfortless picture of a widow who could have done without any reminder of the husband she was rid of. She fingered the book, turning the magnificent pages. 'You shall read to me, Cecily.'

'I cannot read, madam.'

Her aunt frowned. 'Nor write?'

'Oh yes—yes. My name. I can write Cecily Jolland.'

'My brother does nothing by halves. I could read and write when I was nine years old. And so could he— our father would not have it otherwise . . . Well, Cecily Jolland, I shall teach you this as I shall teach you many other things you need to know.'

They went down the narrow stair and out of the house. The afternoon was so full of light that Cecily put up her hand to shield her eyes as she looked out over the wide countryside.

Mantlemass stood on a ridge of ground that stretched east and west almost in a straight line. The house faced towards the south, while northward a hanger of fine beech trees broke the coldest winds. Ahead of the main court-yard, which here was nothing grander than a wide stretch of beaten earth, the ground dropped away in increasingly shallow terraces that looked almost man-made. At last the land flattened into a narrow valley, and there the river ran. On the far side the ground rose again, but only to the west, and a quarter as high. Beyond, the view extended interminably over rolling countryside, half heath, half sprawling woodland that hung like a thick cloak on the shoulders of the hills. On the open ground were great spreads of heather, and among the trees there was already gold enough to prove that summer was passing. On the furthest horizon, barer hills stood against the sky.

'The ocean is beyond,' Dame Elizabeth said. 'It is something over twenty miles. Not too long a ride in good weather. Your mother's daughter should know how to sit a horse—your uncle, Lord Digby, could tell you something of that. Now come this way towards the farm. I shall show you my trade.'

About the farm there was great activity, a number of men coming and going. Each of them Dame Elizabeth called by name, asking after wives and children, receiving replies that were free and friendly, open and without humility. They were her tenants and bound to serve her, but they seemed to regard her with a frankness that Cecily found a little shocking.

The farm had many buildings, the tithe barn biggest of all, but almost matched by its neighbours. All were built of stone, the colour of honey streaked with treacle. It was the local stone, quarried for building in all these parts, but smelted, too, in the nearby furnaces for its iron ore. All these necessary buildings were thatched with fine reeds similar to those used for the floor of the hall.

Dame Elizabeth led the way towards a group of three buildings standing a little apart from the rest. She pushed open a heavy door and went inside. Cecily hesitated to follow, checked by the stench that was so strong she had to clap a hand over her nose and mouth. Her aunt called to her to close the door behind her, and she went in reluctantly. The building was stacked with piles of small dried pelts.

'You see,' Dame Elizabeth said, taking up a pair and shaking them, 'this is my trade, Cecily. I am a skinner, no less. These are coney skins. We breed the coneys in warrens on our own ground—you will see them presently. Rabbits are fine breeders, but they must be contained and kept from the crops. I have a growing trade in these skins. They sell to London for the trimming of mantles and caps. I sell also to France, and to the Low Countries, and to Italy—the fashion is on my side. This is how I prosper.

This is why my hands have hardened, niece—in a manner I see you do not approve. In the next building I shall show you the skins stretched for drying. We pin them and leave them long in the sun before bringing the racks indoors.' She looked at Cecily's wrinkling nose and laughed. 'Yes— the smell is unfortunate. But no more odious than the smell of any other dead animal—including man . . . Ah, you think me sadly coarsened. But you and I will eat and grow fat because I have hardened my hands and my heart and set about my own salvation. It is true I have this manor held from the Crown: one day I may gain the freehold for myself and for my heirs, but meanwhile I depend for my living on myself—and am grateful that I do so.'

As they came into the air again, the redbeard, Henty, was crossing the yard, bringing a small dark man who snatched off his cap the instant he saw Dame Elizabeth, and bowed half a dozen times as he approached her.

'This is the Frenchman who sells my skins across the water,' her aunt told Cecily. 'Where are you going?' For the girl had turned away, pulling at her veil as if she would hide her face. 'And what are you doing? I see I have quite forgotten fashionable ways. We live an honest, open life here. None of us is so bad that he may not look at his neighbour's face—and none too good to be looked at.'

'My father—' began Cecily.

'You must learn to obey me, now. But move apart, if you wish. I have business matters to attend to.' She called out to the little dark man. 'Good day to you. What bills have you brought me?'

Cecily looked about her. Privacy was not easily come by. Wherever she turned she saw people watching her curiously—a boy carrying an armful of skins, a herdsman with a dog at his heels, two dairy maids with pails slung on yokes, an old man chopping wood, and a small, dirty-faced child, who came close, staring. Each of these people looked at her, smiling or solemn, shy or bold, and their interest was almost frightening.

She walked slowly away from the yard. She came over a little brow and there she seemed shut off from prying eyes. A clump of bushes, brambles and gorse, sprawled down the slope and she stepped a few yards that way, feeling at once curious and unnaturally bold. Here there was a spread of grass, cropped close, but clean. She sank down, curling her feet up under her skirts, recalling as she did so how her aunt's skirts swung above her instep like those of any peasant woman, and how freely she walked because of it—yet somehow lost no dignity. Cecily sat frowning in the sunshine, plucking curious and unfamiliar thoughts from a mind that whirled with resentment, with emotion and change.

Although the bustle of the farm continued out of sight, utter stillness held all that she looked out upon from her shelter. Beyond the river the young trees stepped grace-fully up the gentle slope, the ground beneath them cleared and trampled into a firm floor by pigs rooting for acorns. There was no movement now among the trees, but over the little river a heron flapped low and lazy, then dropped to fish. She had watched such birds often from the river-side in her father's London home, and their distance as they settled in the far verges had seemed infinite. The meadows beyond were a world she would never enter, and she had seen no reason why she should. Now, on the slopes of the forest, that first day at Mantlemass, the almost unwelcome thought came to Cecily that she might cross the narrow water here and walk among the trees, if indeed she chose.

A horse came picking its way over the hillside as she watched, slithering every now and again on the narrow track, reins slack on its neck as the rider let the animal find its own way. The rider was a lad in a torn shirt. Cecily could hear him whistling. He had a brown dog with him, nosing and snuffling as it came. The simple picture made by the boy, the dog and the horse filled Cecily with a feeling of warmth and promise—as though there was an ease and contentment in life which she, too, might somehow share.

Her aunt's loud voice behind her made Cecily spring to her feet. Dame Elizabeth was waving her arms, fists clenched, and shouting across the valley at the boy on his horse.

'Lewis! Lewis Mallory! Get that dog off my land! It'll be the worse otherwise! Do you hear me, boy?' Her anger was only mocking, Cecily thought—she sounded as though she would as easily laugh as shout. 'Heed what I say, Lewis Mallory! Off! Be off!'

The boy looked up. He pulled off his red cap and swept it in a low bow that threatened to tip him from the saddle. It was impossible to see his face, but he could only have been grinning. He twitched the horse's head and moved off among the trees, unhurried. Soon the woods had swallowed him.

'Must he not ride here, madam?' Cecily asked, gazing after him.

'The land is mine—though his people claim a right of passage over it. I cannot have dogs there—the mouth of one warren is above the river. Besides—he'll be in trouble if he runs his dog so freely. The verderers and those who should keep the forest for the Crown have grown slack enough—but a new king may stir them up to remember their duties. There are strict laws about the keeping of dogs and hawks.'

'Then why does he ride there?'

'I have told you his people claim they have right of

3

way. It is a short cut from the high road to Ghylls Hatch.
That's the Orlebars' farm, where the boy belongs.'

'You called him by another name,' said Cecily.

'Mallory. Orlebars are cousins to Mallorys, though in
a humble kind.'

The boy had looked humble enough himself, Cecily
thought, with his tattered shirt; she pictured the Orlebars
as crude peasants scratching a living from barren ground;
though both names, Orlebar and Mallory, had a good
Norman ring to them. The boy's gesture, his mocking
bow and refusal to make any haste, went better with his
name than with his clothes.

'Have you heard the name spoken?' her aunt was
asking.

'Orlebar, madam?'

'Mallory . . . No—I see it means nothing to you. Yet
when I chose my new home—and I could have had one
of five manors about England—I chose Mantlemass
because my neighbour's name was known to me.'

Cecily smiled rather loftily—so much concern for such
people . . . 'You make it sound a mystery.'

'Perhaps it is; though not of my making . . . Come
indoors, now.'

'But pray—unravel the mystery first.'

'I may not have the means.'

'Then tell me the parts of the riddle,' Cecily urged,
frowning and impatient.

'Not now. But keep your heart up. It is almost certain
we shall both see the solution one of these days.'

3
Mallory and Orlebar

As soon as he was out of sight of Mantlemass, Lewis whistled up his dog and got on his way. He was still grinning to himself at Dame Elizabeth's furious shouts, for he had known her a long time—her bark was ferocious but her bite was practically unknown. He had been only ten years old when she came to Mantlemass and he to Ghylls Hatch. They had met for the first time when she found him crying in the forest because he had decided to run away from his cousin's house, and he had lost himself almost immediately. First she had scoffed at his tears, then she had called him a coward; and then she had told him to run back quickly to Ghylls Hatch on the path she would show him, for she would like to know that she was to have him for her neighbour. That was something he had never forgotten—people seldom spoke so reasonably and kindly to a mere child. There were many miserable moments during that first year in his cousin's household, but he did not think of running away again. Dame Elizabeth never came to Ghylls Hatch without asking for him and they had fallen into a teasing way together—so that when she bellowed at him he knew her shouts could easily turn to laughter, and when he defied her and flouted her orders they both knew that he would never do anything to distress or harm her . . . It was said that Dame Elizabeth's niece had come to Mantlemass now, and that might have been the girl he had noticed standing beside her as she shouted to him about the dog. A girl in a rich gown that looked strange, if not ridiculous, next to Dame Elizabeth's homespun.

He rode on along the familiar track, Mantlemass and Mantlemass land away behind him and the open pastures that surrounded Ghylls Hatch opening up to the north. There were six colts in the bottom enclosure, tearing in wide and wider circles, their manes and tails flying. It would be his job and his pleasure to take a hand in breaking them when the time came. Skittish as they were now, they showed already some sign of the deep-chested weight carriers they would become. Lewis Mallory's cousin Orlebar bred horses for battle and for jousting, a profession he had inherited from his father. For his own pleasure, he also bred swifter animals for the chase. If a lad was obliged to leave his own home, his parents and his brother, and come to a new way of life, then none was better than this one; Lewis was quite certain of that by now. And because to recall the past baffled and disturbed him, it often seemed as if his life had begun somewhere about his tenth birthday.

'But why must I come here? Why must I stay?' he had cried in despair in those early days.

'You are to be my heir,' his cousin had replied.

And the boy had looked round Ghylls Hatch and seen only a meagre inheritance, thinking of how much would have been his if he had not been inexplicably passed over by his father in favour of his younger brother . . . Nowadays he looked at the horses, at the broad acres won over the years from the forest, and his fortune seemed fair enough. . . .

'Pick up your feet, you sloven!' he told Diamante, as she pecked at the hillside. He put her into a canter, calling again to the dog, and the three of them made quick work of the last mile home.

When Lewis rode into the yard, Master Orlebar was in the stables with a lame mare. He emerged with a long face, saying the animal would be good for nothing after this and might as well have her throat cut, for the tendon was hopelessly damaged.

'She'll make a good brood,' Lewis said.

'She was bred for the chase.'

'Even so. We can put her to Ebony or Duke and she'll more than make her keep.'

'She was bred for the chase, boy.'

'And so shall her progeny be,' insisted Lewis, every bit as stubborn as his cousin.

At this Roger Orlebar laughed a little, for he and Lewis had come to understand one another very well.

'How if I give her to you?'

'Give her to me? Give me Iris?' Lewis sounded incredulous. 'If you truly mean that, cousin—'

'I do. I do. It is time you had your own responsibilities. Not that I mean you to neglect mine in consequence.'

'When I sell my first foal I'll pay you back her keep,' Lewis promised. 'And then the line shall be mine for ever after.'

Now Orlebar was laughing deeply from his big throat.

He was a short square man, black-with-grey about the hair and beard, with surprising blue eyes that looked too mild for his disposition, and a certain modesty, or shyness, in his manner. He had proved a good substitute for a father, though he had no sons of his own. His father having been a gentleman who wilfully chose country ways, Roger Orlebar had been brought up here in the forest and had never been sent out into the world for his education, as a gentleman's son should be. He was an unsuitable husband for any bride his father had considered worthy, and too proud himself to marry a country girl. His sister Jenufer kept his house, at least nominally. But she was so simple as to be spoken of as half-witted.

She was coming from the kitchen as Lewis went indoors. Ghylls Hatch consisted of a straggle of buildings, and the family lived in the largest, a small yeoman's dwelling that had been put in order by Roger Orlebar's father. The place was ill-cared for, but since there was no true lady of the house, nobody noticed this. The same rushes lay on the floor from year's end to year's end.

Jenufer, a tiny wispy woman older than her brother but girlish, often distressingly so, in her manner, was in her good mood today—a pleasant alternative to those days when she wandered about the house weeping, tears pouring, but making no sound. She ran to Lewis and seized his hands and shook them up and down.

'Where have you been, my lovely boy?'

'Past Mantlemass.' He stooped and kissed her cheek. 'Dame Elizabeth shouted at me. She had a stranger at her side.'

'My brother says her niece has come to stay. And she screamed and fought and bit because she had no wish to remain there. Anis Bostel came from Mantlemass with a cheese, and she said it was so.'

'She did not look as though she would bite, Cousin

Jenufer. I think you have been nabbling, you and the Mantlemass reeve's wife.'

'Well, I shall never speak with the girl,' said Jenufer, sticking up her chin and pursing her lips, 'for her family and ours have disagreements.'

'Her family? Her father can only be Dame Elizabeth's brother. We have no disagreements with her.'

'Well, this girl—this girl's father . . .' Jenufer began to look troubled and her voice tailed off into a murmur. 'I cannot recall his name. He is—who? I cannot tell at all. It has quite gone from my mind . . . Oh how shall I remember?'

'There,' Lewis said, 'what does it matter?' He hated to see her worried. 'It is nothing to the point,' he assured her. 'Not near so much as brushing your hair like a lady, cousin. And where is your cap? What a mawkin you look, to be sure.'

'I'll do it,' she said. 'Now.' And she ran away quickly, as light as a girl.

Roger Orlebar had come into the house, and he watched his sister run away.

'She should have a new gown for winter,' he said. 'Poor blessed soul, I am a sad brother to her, always forgetting her needs. I'll see about some yarn and you shall ride with it to the weaver. One of the maids can cut and stitch the cloth when it's done—Susan is neatest and cleanest. Ah, poor Jenufer—poor Jenufer. What a burden!'

When they had done with supper, Roger Orlebar sat at the cleared table, peering by rushlight at his bills of accounting, that he read with difficulty and calculated with much reckoning on his fingers. Lewis escaped before he could be called upon to help.

The night was clear with a moon moving into the second quarter. Lewis took the track that ran south and west from Ghylls Hatch. He felt elated by the business of the mare and he came very quickly to the priest's house by the old, half-ruined, palace. Though it was called a palace it was in fact a hunting lodge; but kings had come there to hunt and so made the place royal. The chapel, however, was maintained in good shape, thanks largely to the chaplain. It was a curious benefice. Day by day the priest, Sir James, said mass in the chapel and performed every office of the holy calendar. Sometimes his congregation was two or three; sometimes there was none but himself to pray. If he was free of work at the right hour, Lewis would serve mass for him. This was a man he respected and loved quite beyond his priestly importance. The priest was long past middle life but carried his years buoyantly. He had thick white hair and a skin browned by all weathers. He lived off his own bit of land, tithes from his few parishioners—these were contested by the parish priest of the church in the village four miles or so away—and the venison which was a perquisite of his office; he could take two bucks a year for himself, and he would enjoy the meat fresh until he sickened of it, cure what he could by smoking it in his own chimney, and give the rest to the needy.

Sir James had taken upon himself to give Lewis some sort of learning. He had taught him to read, to write, to calculate; to name the stars; to watch the life of the forest, bird and plant and animal, and to interpret the science of heraldry. He had also taught him to forgive injustice, to accept a humble place in life without rancour, to play the lute and recorder, and to sing.

'You are my choir, my deacon and my pupil,' the priest often told Lewis. 'I should have had a poor time of it, these years, if you had not been sent to me.'

So this evening he was glad to see Lewis, and drew him to sit by the fire immediately.

'And what have you done through the length of this fine day, my son?'

'Worked before noon, worked afternoon, rid in late afternoon, and ate my supper like a grateful Christian . . . The best news is—my cousin has given me the chestnut mare, Iris—that went so lame—and I am to breed from her for my own profit. So this day is important, Father. I have become a man of affairs.'

'And does that mean you will stay the rest of your days at Ghylls Hatch as your cousin Orlebar has done? And see nothing of the world?'

'It might be so.'

'You are the son of a noble and prosperous gentleman, Lewis. Is it enough for you to stay a forester?'

'You will recall that the noble and prosperous gentleman disowned me and preferred my brother. I am content with what I have. I have forgotten ten years. Yes, Father it is enough to stay a forester. Though I'll not stay a bachelor, like my cousin. A country girl can make me a good enough wife, I daresay. I am past seventeen and should be thinking where to seek her.'

'There is no hurry,' Sir James said.

Lewis laughed. He did not see many girls and was wary of those he did see—at farms and cottages about the forest, and in church on Sundays, not at the palace chapel, but in the village. Some of these were so lumpish he could not tolerate the thought of them. But some had charm. Master Urry, who smelted iron over in the south-east corner of the forest, had three shy flaxen-haired daughters, and he had kissed the youngest last Christmas, in the dark, as they left the church after the first mass of the day. And there was a girl at the mill he had admired— though his cousin Jenufer assured him she was no better than she should be.

'When I have chosen a wife,' Lewis said, 'none but you shall marry us.'

'There is no hurry,' the priest said again, frowning

slightly. And he began to speak of other things, of forest matters, of the determination of that same Master Urry to use a great hammer driven by water to beat out his iron; and how he had been laughed at by those who went to work less ambitiously. 'The skills they're happy with have barely changed since the days of the Romans,' Sir James said.

'Will it work—the big hammer?' Lewis wondered.

'Not there, where he is trying. The water is too little, and the ground too flat. But I wish him well of his ambitions. Though it will make a devilish enough noise when he succeeds.'

'That'll enrage Dame Elizabeth,' Lewis said. 'Already she complains of the noise—and that's beating by hand.' He grinned as he spoke of her. 'We all say the same, father —do you notice? How will this seem to Dame Elizabeth? What will Dame Elizabeth do? Beware of Dame Elizabeth! She rules the forest, it seems to me.'

'A fine woman who might well be a bitter one. A hard life, my son—she has had a hard life. Her tongue may be sharp but she is a good friend when a friend is needed.'

'I know it,' Lewis said. 'How was her life hard?' He often tried to trip the priest into confidences and rarely succeeded, but tonight Sir James spoke out because he wished to defend Dame Elizabeth. He said she had suffered a sad marriage.

'You mean she has no children—and that has caused her sadness?'

'Women can seldom choose how their lives shall be lived. She was wed to a man of some standing . . . Lewis Mallory, this is title-tattle—I'm being a nabbler, as these people say.'

'A man of some standing—but . . . ?'

'Well, there is no secret in it. FitzEdmund. The name speaks for itself. He was royally connected—but not in wedlock. He had his own misfortunes—a crooked back besides a crooked birth, and no doubt these things worked on him. We must not judge him—but he was a cruel man.'

'Was it her father made her wed?' the boy asked.

'Her ambitious brother . . . Lewis, that is all I may say. It will be forgiven me, for it excuses some harshness in her.'

'They say her niece has come to Mantlemass. Is she the daughter of that same ambitious brother? Then what may he have in store for her?'

He remembered the girl standing on the edge of the farmyard in her fine clothes. He had little occasion to think fondly of his own father—but at least he seemed free to choose whom he would marry.

'Take the lute,' said Sir James, putting an end to the conversation, 'and I will have the recorder. We'll have some music to send you home tranquil—and it must be soon, or you'll find the door barred against you.'

It was some time before Roger Orlebar obtained yarn for his sister's gown. Lewis would take it to the weaver, who was to dye it, for there was none more skilled than he in this particular.

'And let it be a fine purplish mulberry,' Jenufer decided. 'Now tell him my wishes, cousin—a fine mulberry I must have.'

'Then mulberry it shall be,' Lewis said. 'But when it comes home you must promise not to expect saffron, or scarlet, or blue.'

'I never change my mind,' she said positively, 'and that you should know as well as I do.'

There had been rain at night in the past weeks and this had advanced the season. Soon the coloured leaves would fall to the first frost, the bracken, already gold, would flame before it died. The preparation for winter, proceeding steadily from the harvest, would speed to a frenzy against the first snowfall that so often came before Christmas, gripping the forest for a week or more before releasing it until the severe and lasting falls of January. The weaver's cottage was a few miles from Ghylls Hatch, set halfway up a shallow bank and approached across a ford. The stream was only four feet wide and very gentle. Lower down it was dammed and slid over a gushing weir into a pool. Here the weaver, Halacre—or Halfacre, according to some—bleached, shrank and tented his stuff on pegged frames.

Halfway between Ghylls Hatch and the weaver's cottage there was a track that ran double, the one part three or four feet higher than the other, with a screen of trees between. Lewis rode on the higher track, idling because the day was fine. It was some time before he caught a glimpse of riders on the lower path. He heard a woman's voice—indisputably that of Dame Elizabeth FitzEdmund. Occasionally a lighter, softer voice replied—lighter and softer, but a little sullen. Lewis was too curious to forego the privilege of eavesdropping.

It was soon apparent that he was not the only one taking yarn to the weaver.

'It shall be a russet red,' Dame Elizabeth was saying, 'for this is a colour at which he excels. A warm colour for winter, too. That reminds me, niece, that the cloak you rode in when you came from London is not heavy enough for our winter.'

'I shall stay indoors,' said the girl.

'I could spare skins enough to line the hood and shoulders,' Dame Elizabeth said, ignoring the reply. 'Perhaps even a little more. Second-quality fur, but very well for such a purpose.' Then she paused and waited, but the girl said nothing. 'At least,' said her aunt very drily, 'I will do it if you will thank me.'

'I do thank you, madam,' murmured the girl.

'But today is a black day with you, and so you wish to punish me for being thoughtful!'

'No, madam.'

'*Yes*, madam,' said Dame Elizabeth.

Lewis nearly laughed aloud. He rode very carefully and Diamante seemed to sense his caution, for she trod so lightly no twig snapped to betray them. The two women remained unaware that they were overlooked, though sometimes Lewis was quite close, peering down at them through the trees whose leaves had conveniently thinned. The girl was riding a rough little chestnut mare that had gone to Mantlemass from Ghylls Hatch a year or two previously—Cressyd was her name. The girl rode gracefully, straight-backed and light-handed. Country women rode like bundles, Lewis always complained, or else they never stirred except pillion behind their husbands or their fathers or their sons. Cressyd was quite a pretty little creature, though she was poorly groomed at present, but the boy decided that her rider deserved a better mount. The idea pleased him. He would see if he could persuade Dame Elizabeth to let her niece try the beautiful grey Zephyr, the finest of them all.

Lewis kept his distance, and when the weaver's cottage came into view, he hung back behind the screening trees to watch. Dame Elizabeth moved swiftly on a track long familiar, but the girl followed more warily until her aunt looked back and called. Then she hurried—but Lewis could tell from the set of her shoulders that she was in a bad humour. Poor thing—she was a stranger here, and he could remember what that meant, though for him it was long past. He watched her pick her way across the ford, then speed Cressyd up the hillside. Though she was in a bad humour she showed none of it in her treatment of the little chestnut, and Lewis warmed to her. Dame Elizabeth was already calling to the weaver and he came hurrying to greet her. It was noticeable that he did so without any humility. He laid his hand on her bridle and looked up smiling and confident. These forest people, Lewis knew, had no fear of the lady of Mantlemass, whether or not they were her tenants. Her brusque manner, her loud commanding voice that was none the less without arrogance, was acceptable to them—they respected her firmness because it went hand in hand with fairness.

'We have brought you an autumn task,' she was saying to the weaver. 'Your best weaving for the best sort of yarn. Let me see what dyes you have at present.'

'Come to the vats, lady,' he said. 'You know the way as I do.'

She dismounted while he held the horse's head, then instead of tethering the creature she tossed the rein to her niece, who had now reached her side. The girl's astonishment was obvious—she might as well have spoken aloud: *Does she think I am her groom?* But she said nothing, and sat like a statue, holding big Farden as she had been bidden. At this short distance Lewis could see that her fine gown had become very draggled about the hem. Her veil showed signs of having been roughly fingered by branches and briars, but it would have filled any local maid with envy. She still looked too grand for any country lad to speak to without fawning. On a leather thong round his neck, hidden in his shirt, Lewis wore a ring engraved with his family crest. He had stolen it from his father's closet on the day he was sent from home—and he wished he might display it to prove his quality.

He prodded Diamante and in his turn rode over the little river. He knew the girl was watching and he made his approach up the hillside a showy affair, bringing Diamante prettily on to her haunches before leaping from the saddle.

He stood for a fraction of a second, wondering whether to conclude the gesture by asking her to hold his horse, since she was holding one already; but he had not quite the impertinence to do it. He contented himself with snatching off his red cap, bowing extravagantly, and calling 'God save you, lady.' He tied up Diamante and went striding on and into the cottage after Dame Elizabeth. He had to stoop at the door, not because he was unusually tall, but because it was a mean entry. Turning his back on the girl he was conscious that his leather jerkin was slit across the shoulders where he had broadened over the last six months or so.

Dame Elizabeth and the weaver had passed through the cottage to where six or eight vats of dye stood under a thatched lean-to shelter, or cove.

'The russet,' Dame Elizabeth was saying, and she handed her yarn to the weaver, nodding to Lewis.

'The russet, then, it shall be,' he said. 'And what for you, Lewis Mallory?'

'A mulberry. It is for my cousin Jenufer.'

'How does that poor soul fare?' Dame Elizabeth asked.

'I think as usual, madam. Neither sad nor gay for long.'

'I shall come visiting shortly. I have business to discuss with Master Orlebar. I need marl for my fields from the Ghylls Hatch pits, and I think he will spare it to me.'

'I know he will,' Lewis answered. 'Shall it be your men to dig it, or ours?'

'It shall be mine,' said Dame Elizabeth firmly, far too good a business woman, as he very well knew, to add to the price by employing another man's labour. 'And tell your cousin that my man, Nicholas Forge, has been about my accounts in London, and the talk there is all of the new king and the new ways. Riding home, he met with the forest reeve—by spring or summer there's to be a survey of all royal parks and chases, of freeholds and copyholds and cattle. So tell your cousin we must all look to our boundaries and stand firm for our rights.'

'I'll tell him, madam,' Lewis promised. Then he handed the weaver his hanks of yarn for Jenufer's new gown.

'No more than a quarter as fine as what our good lady has brought me,' Halacre grumbled, fingering the yarn and pulling a long face. 'There'll be nubbles in the cloth, most likely. Bad spinning—though the texture of the wool's fairly suent.'

'Do your best, then.'

'Surely. A bit of good sewing after I've done my part, and the lady shall look gimsy enough.'

'As gimsy as the maid at your door, weaver,' said Lewis, since Dame Elizabeth by now was moving on her way and should be out of earshot.

'That's a poor pretty thing and no mistake,' the weaver replied. 'Too delicate for these parts and I can only pray she'll settle.'

'How long will she stay?'

'That none knows. They say her father's gone into France. He was the last king's man, they say.'

'Who told you so?'

'I do forget that, percizely,' the weaver said.

He stood at Lewis's side and they looked out through the cottage to the sunshine on the far side. In the frame of the small doorway they saw Dame Elizabeth mounting and riding away, and the girl following. She glanced back once over her shoulder, then moved out of sight.

'She see you,' said the weaver. He looked up into Lewis's face and laughed gently.

4
Her Aunt's Niece

Weeks ago Cecily had grown sick of her London gown,
with its dirty hem. Fine-lady clothes seemed increasingly
out of place as she watched her aunt so free among her
tenants and her house servants. The forest was not such
an unpeopled desert after all—only it was dwelt in by
such as she would not have supposed worth any notice.
She listened to Dame Elizabeth talking to Anis Bostle,
the reeve's wife, about her children; discussing the horses
with Simon Carter, to whom they were his family;
enquiring of Nicholas Forge on his return from London
if he had met with his sister while he was away, and how
was her marriage going? It was not only coneys and coney
skins and orders for distant places that Dame Elizabeth

4

talked over with red-haired Henty—she was concerned
for his only son, born blind, for his daughter who cared
for the boy since their mother was dead, and how she had
been asked in marriage but would not leave her father and
brother to be looked after by strangers. Janet in the dairy
would never go home to visit her mother because she
boxed her ears; Meg cried because nobody seemed
anxious to marry her; Goody Ann had lost her last tooth
and must be especially cared for . . . a need to become a
part of all this stirred and grew in Cecily, and it was her
unsuitable dress that seemed to isolate her. It must be
weeks before the cloth could be fetched from the weaver. . . .

'Perhaps, madam,' she said at last awkwardly to her
aunt, 'there is some old gown of your own that could be
made to fit me . . . ' She looked quickly at Dame Elizabeth,
who however showed no sign of finding the suggestion
unusual. She did not raise her eyebrows, nor smile in a
manner that would seem to say: *so you have come to your
senses*.

'There's a blue wool that might serve,' she said.
'Somewhere about the colour of your own. I'll see how it
is.'

Cecily had asked for the gown, but when it was cut
down to her size the rather faded blue disgusted her. She
plucked at the neck, finding it harsh against her skin. She
thought of Alys, of the silks and the velvets that had
come to her father's house, bales and bales brought by
merchants because Sir Thomas Jolland had a name for
loving fine things. These men would be waiting somewhere in the outer quarters while Alys looped and draped
the stuff, sweeping and strutting across the floor to show
off the folds . . . Cecily put her hands to her face, hungry
for the memory of Alys who—sly-eyed or no—had made
her feel she could do no wrong. . . .

'Be still a moment,' said Mary Butterwick, who was

measuring the hem of the blue dress. 'Else, I'll get it
curly as a shepherd's crook.'

Cecily looked down and saw her feet and ankles uncovered for all the world to stare at.

'Too short! It's too short!'

'Longer, it'll trail in the gubber,' Mary said.

'Lord, girl, talk Christian talk or be silent! *Gubber*
makes no sense to me.'

'Gubber's stoach,' explained Mary patiently.

'I can't tell a word you speak!' Yet *stoach* did seem to
explain itself. 'If you mean mud, why can't you say so?'

'That'll be spilt with a long hem,' said Mary, beginning
to flush and stammer as she strove to make herself clear.

'*Spilt?*'

'Stoach—I mean mud, lady—mud'll spoil it,' Mary
managed.

Cecily again considered the hemline and her own feet.
The feet looked distressingly sturdy. The display of ankle
was appalling. If her father saw her now he would surely
beat her for immodesty . . . But he could not see her. He
would not be back to see her yet, that was sure. There
was a great deal he must do before he could send for her to
join him—wherever he might be. Why—it could be a
year, two years. Perhaps he would never come, finding
more important things to do, glad to be rid of her . . .
She could not cast off years of closely ordered upbringing
to say she was glad to be rid of him—that would be a
dreadful thing for any daughter. But she was glad to be
rid of the fear that he caused her—to be without that was
almost to be re-born.

The feel of the hem swishing against her ankles gave
Cecily a sudden sensation of daring, of freedom, and as
she pictured herself in her imagination—striding slightly,
in imitation of her aunt—all thoughts of Alys and of her
father's return became unimportant.

'Very well,' she said. 'Stitch it, then. I am in the country now and I must forget courtly ways.'

This grand expression and the manner in which she made it, sighing gracefully, letting her hands hang limply away from her body, caused Mary Butterwick to look awed and respectful.

'And did you see the court, then, lady?'

'Of course. Often,' said Cecily, not quite truthfully, for she had been once only. Something at the time had angered her father—Alys said it was that too many gallants admired her—and after that he had kept her closer than ever before. 'The ladies at court wear tall head-dresses like butterflies' wings, Mary. Gold thread is stitched into their veils. Their foreheads are high and smooth—except when the hair grows again that they have carefully plucked out.'

'Never so!' cried Mary, sitting back on her heels. 'Plucked out? I'd bawl with the pain! Oh you quite frit me, you do indeed! You never did so heathen a thing yourself, that I trust?'

'Maybe—and maybe not,' said Cecily. She remembered the time she had set Alys to plucking out the hair. The tears streamed from her eyes at every tweak, till she was sobbing with pain and Alys refused to go on. 'And how am I to wear my hair now, Mary Butterwick?' she demanded. 'Will you stitch me a cap like yours?'

'This evening, I will—if the mistress allow me a light.'

The dress and the cap were ready by next morning. Now grown accustomed to looking after herself, Cecily was soon into the dress. Then she tried the white linen cap. Mary's covered all her hair but a few reddish curls that hung out on the nape of her neck. Cecily's fitted very snugly, fastening under the chin, but her long fair hair hung free down her back, for there was too much of it to conceal. It made her nervous to leave it uncovered but there was nothing else to be done. She wished she could see how she looked. At home in her father's house she had had a looking glass of her own, but she had seen none at Mantlemass; no doubt her aunt despised such vanity. She looked down at the woollen dress, at the hem swinging above such shoes as she had never worn before. The cobbler in the village had made them skilfully enough, but they felt heavy as lead after the deerskin slippers she was accustomed to.

It was time to go down to prayers. Goody Ann was already ringing the paternoster bell that hung by the big studded door. The door would be standing open and there would be entering a whole crowd of people Cecily now knew by name—the Bostels and their children; Henty and his daughter; the secretary, Nicholas Forge, with his old mother, and all the maids and indoor servants. But those who worked outside, the herdsmen and Sim Carter and the dairymaids and all the rest—always slipped in by the small side door and stood against the wall. There it was to be hoped that the blessings asked for would still fall on them.

Cecily stood some time at her door, listening. She had by now become accustomed to moving about among a number of people, but this morning she had a new face, a new Cecily Jolland to present to them all. An angry shyness overwhelmed her and she had to force herself down the stairs. She went as quickly as possible to take her place beside her aunt.

'God bless you, my child,' said Dame Elizabeth, quite gently. Her glance flicked over the blue gown, the white cap, the long fair hair. She turned her attention to conducting her household's devotions. After the last *Amen* she gave them her orders for the day. 'Now come with me, niece,' she said.

They went out of the hall and across the yard in the

bright early morning. Dame Elizabeth made for the dairy.
The maids were ahead of her and there was a fine noise
and argument going on, for there was a shortage of salt.
Each girl furiously blamed the other, but silence fell when
the mistress of the house walked in.

'You must use the salt set aside for herrings. Go to
the kitchen and ask Moll Thomsett for the crock—and
say I sent you if you want to save yourself from her sharp
tongue. You, Agnes Bunce—you're the strongest to carry
the crock.' Agnes rushed away, and then Dame Elizabeth
said to Cecily, 'Today Janet shall teach you how to churn
butter.'

Cecily had been ready, so she thought, to please her
aunt if possible. But at this indignity she was filled with
black rage.

'Maybe I am your countrified niece, madam; but I am no
dairy maid.'

'Nor I. Yet I can do as I command others, I thank
heaven.'

'You have put me into country clothes,' cried Cecily,
'and now I see why. I am to be your servant!'

'You asked for the plain gown. And I have plenty of
servants.'

'Then let them churn, for I will not.'

'Bread can always be eaten dry.' said Dame Elizabeth,
quitting the dairy.

Cecily saw Janet looking at her open-mouthed. 'Don't
stare, girl!' she snapped. She ran out of the dairy and hid
inside the nearest barn while she fought with tears of
fury. Yet these, if indeed they fell, would be less painful
tears than any she had shed since babyhood. Like a
scared animal that is rigid in despair, then turns on those
who have caged it, Cecily's spirit was rising. Not only
her appearance had changed, but her thoughts and her
impulses—how had she dared speak to her aunt as she

had just done? She knew she had to ask forgiveness, and she ran out of the barn and almost went ankle deep into a puddle spreading where the churns had been swilled out with spring water. The sun turned the puddle into the mirror she lacked and looking down Cecily saw herself reflected, head to toe. She saw a stranger. She stood there looking and looking, not at her father's daughter—but at her aunt's niece. It was all too clear, as she watched the scowl gradually easing from her reflected face, how her apology should be offered.

She struggled against the necessity, beating her clenched fists together painfully. But there was no escape from her conscience. She went slowly but firmly back to the dairy, slamming open the door with her last flare of resentment.

At last it was time to go to the weaver to enquire after the russet cloth. Cecily should go herself, Dame Elizabeth said.

'Who shall go with me?'

'You know the way.'

'I cannot—' began Cecily; then paused. They were in the barn where the skins were sorted. Cecily looked sideways at her aunt, who was weighing a batch of skins, one against the other, for pricing. There was a rhythm to the work as the skins were tossed into two heaps, the good and the indifferent. 'Do you mean I should ride alone, madam?'

'What do you fear?' With a piece of chalkstone Dame Elizabeth marked each pelt before throwing it on to its appropriate heap.

'It is not that I *fear* . . .' murmured Cecily.

'But you think a gentlewoman should not ride abroad unattended. What have I told you? We live differently here. Treat the forest as your own parkland. Be a woman,

Cecily,' she said—much as a father might say to his son:
Be a man.

Cecily said no more. Part of her hesitation was less a
matter of convention than of sheer incredulity. It seemed
impossible that such things should happen to her. Some
time after noon she herself asked Simon Carter to saddle
up Cressyd. It was the first time she had ever given an
order in her own behalf.

'I am to ride to Halacre, the weaver,' she said, waiting
to see if Simon frowned or looked astonished, as any
servant of her father's would have done.

'And a good day for it,' he replied. 'Cressyd know her
way. Not like old Farden, now. He's a sworly beggar and a
proper scambler.'

Cecily had no idea what that meant, but she smiled
and the man smiled back. He brought the mare round
himself and helped her to mount. She moved off at once
towards the forest track that led two miles or so to the
weaver's cottage.

The scene was changing. There had been several sharp
frosts and today there was a keen wind blowing from the
south-east. At the head of the track Cecily pulled in her
horse. She was moving into a different world where she
would no longer be protected but must rely upon herself.
If she lost her way—then she must find it again. If the
horse stumbled and threw her, then she must pick herself
up and re-mount—and no one would cry out that the
horse had been at fault. Ever since she had changed her
gown and learnt to walk in hard shoes, and had handled a
churn in the dairy, Cecily had become each day bolder.
But this journey alone was the culmination of her new
experiences. As she hesitated, looking down the track, she
knew that once having ridden out by herself, she would
have enjoyed something it would be almost impossible to
forego. As she accepted this thought she accepted another

—that in the house by London's river she had lived like a painted, tottering image of a girl, while here she might one day become herself. *She shall be happy here as never in her life before*—that was what her aunt had said to Friar Paul. And it could be true. But for how long?

She twitched the bridle, twitching away her doubts as she did so. Cressyd moved off at once. The track immediately descended and curved a little towards the south. The house, the farm and all that lived and moved about them were snatched from view. Ahead the heath opened up briefly, then melted into true forest. More than half the leaves were down now and beneath the beeches the ground was as bright as the trees' highest tops. The bracken by the side of the track looked as if it had caught sparks from that blaze and broken into flame. Briefly, as the horse descended towards the trees there was the sound of metal on metal, ugly and powerful. Then that receded and was finally carried away. Robins sang piercingly among the scrub.

In the stillness and silence of the hollow in which she found herself, Cecily heard this song and the small sounds of birds calling in alarm at her passing, shifting among the branches, flying like arrows above her head. Cressyd pricked her ears as a rabbit bolted out of the bracken and away with a strong *pad pad* of hard-clawed feet on dry ground. Horse and rider, content together, moved along the narrow bottom, then jogged gently up the next incline, coming out above a second valley. They were still sheltered from the wind and the sounds it carried, but here the river gushed noisily, dropping loudly and lustily over sharp edges of rock, then spreading into pools. Riding down the bank side, Cecily could see the water winking among the shifting branches of small trees, almost leafless now.

Then she heard a new sound. Down by the pool

someone was whistling quietly. She paused. Curiosity was still new to her. She gave it its head as she gave Cressyd hers.

She was almost certain who she would find.

Alongside the pool Lewis had paused to see if his old friend and enemy, a fine brown trout, had got through the summer and was facing the winter in good health. He was on his way to the forge in the village, to find the smith and beg a day of his time for Ghylls Hatch. Their own man was sick, coughing so badly that he seemed unlikely to recover. The fine afternoon was too good to waste on nothing but a working-day errand and to spin it out Lewis had chosen to walk. This pool in its clearing, with the young surrounding trees to make it private, had always been one of his delights. It was near enough home to take away any feeling of truancy, and far enough away for no one to know where he was. It was his place, his own, where seldom another soul passed by. So that he broke off whistling and leapt up in a rage when he heard a horse on the track. Then he recognised Cressyd and after that her rider.

Lewis pulled off his red cap and stood waiting. He was silent but smiling now. He stood easily, and Cecily would have said he looked more like one of the young squires she had watched serving their masters at her father's table than like the countryman he seemed to be. He watched Cressyd picking her way down the track. Then he saw how the girl was changed, her fine clothes gone, her hair down her back, her veils exchanged for a plain linen cap. Yet she retained some difference, and in a way they both looked strangers to this place. He accepted that she was a stranger, but she did not know yet, he presumed, that he had not been born and spent all his years on the forest.

'A good day to you,' he said, as she came near. 'You're bringing the mare to drink, I see.'

'Yes,' she said. He was not to know that this was the first time she had ever spoken to a stranger, and the first time she had found herself unattended in the presence of man or boy. Or that she was finding it a good deal less alarming than she had been led to expect.

'There's shallow water this end of the pool,' he said. 'Take care—the brambles. If you dismount I'll lead the mare to a good place.'

He came to her side, took the bridle and held out his hand. When she dismounted he led Cressyd away, slipping the bridle over a jut of stone so that the mare had ample freedom to drink if she chose.

'Are you going to the weaver's?' he asked.

'Do you know everything?' She sounded amused and condescending.

'As much as the next man—we all know one another's business. There's not much Dame Elizabeth FitzEdmund can do that's not talked of about the forest in a matter of hours. That's country living for you.'

She had sat down on a boulder when he spread his jerkin for her. She seemed to listen to him intently. He liked her grey eyes and dark lashes, but he was irritated by her clipped and finicky way of speaking—it was as though she held her voice and her tongue like little dogs on tight leashes. As for him, he knew he might seem uncouth to her. He had the same roll in his speech as anyone else in these parts, though he seldom used their outlandish words.

'It's a full two-month since I came to Mantlemass,' she said—and he almost jumped at the change, for she had dropped her voice several tones. He gave her a sharp glance, looking for mockery; but there was none in her expression now. 'That's a long while,' she said.

'Why did you come?' he asked.

'To visit my aunt—why else?'

'They say your father left you because of matters he must attend to in foreign parts.'

'And so he did,' she agreed, now looking down at her hands. And she added, but he thought with little longing in her voice, 'And shall return to fetch me.'

Lewis narrowed his eyes. 'Is your father a king's man?'

'It's King Henry now.'

'Then is he King Henry's man?'

She fidgeted under this and seemed to seek about for some way of escape. 'When my father was at court, it was King Richard.'

'Well, some had to be for York or there'd have been nothing to fight about,' he said reasonably. He wanted to help her. He remembered his cousin Jenufer had spoken slightingly of her father, and mad or not she sometimes knew more than would have been expected. 'I daresay you would not have him change. Fidelity is what matters. He is best abroad, therefore, and you must bear it.'

'I do bear it.' She was blushing slightly now. 'Fetch the mare,' she said.

He smiled and said he would see her on her journey. 'You have come a little out of your way, so I'll set you right.'

'Where's your horse?'

'I'll walk at your stirrup, lady,' he said courteously.

'If you wish it,' she said, sounding a little haughty; but she still spoke in the new, easy voice and seemed pleased by his offer.

He helped her to mount and kept his hand on the bridle. They moved off along the narrow track. Lewis walked politely bare-headed, his red cap tucked into his belt.

'Men hereabouts always favour the House of Lancaster,'

he said, still anxious to put her at her ease. 'It is natural
enough. You know what all this forest is called? It is the
free chase of Lancaster Great Park.' He laughed. 'That
means that the only people free to hunt the game are
kings and princes and nobles—by law, that is. But it's
a long time since any king rode this way and the reeve
and the rangers are foresters by birth—better friends to
other foresters than to their masters, I'd say. All these
acres were given to a one-time Duke of Lancaster. He
was the king's son. It was King Edward, then. The third
of the name.'

'You know a great deal.'

'Your aunt will have spoken of Sir James—he is priest
at the palace chapel. And my tutor. He knows everything
that is past. It was that Duke of Lancaster named Gaunt.
John Gaunt, I think. But we mostly call the place by its
other name—older or newer, that I can't say: Ashdown.'

'What palace?' She frowned. 'Can there be a palace
here?'

'Up on the high ridge. The roof's in. Now there's a
new king and the wars are over, maybe they'll mend it
and come hunting again.'

He had led her back on to the main track and now they
were rising up out of the valley. When they came to the
summit of the next bank he would be able to point out
the weaver's place and continue on his own errand. As
they mounted to the skyline the wind caught them, and
the noise of the iron workings suddenly clamoured at their
ears. It was an ugly sound, yet robust and powerful.

'That'll be the big hammer at Master Urry's,' Lewis
told his companion. 'It's only half successful, I'm told.
The Romans worked iron there once.'

'Who?' she asked, looking very puzzled.

'Did you never hear how the Romans came and took
this country and ruled it?'

'I know nothing of that,' she said.

'Well, so it was; and that is history. But it matters very little,' he assured her, for she was looking very vexed by all this knowledge coming from a countryman. 'I would not know it if Sir James had not told me.' He suddenly jerked on the bridle, checking the mare so sharply that her rider swayed in the saddle and cried out in surprise. 'I thought an adder crossed. But it's already too cold for such creatures. Strangers must beware of them in warmer weather. And in rainy weather they should beware of the bogs—they fill up and become treacherous. But that is chiefly a winter danger, and winter is not yet arrived.'

'What else?' she asked.

'What other dangers? None that I can think of. The deer run in a fair-sized herd and you must keep away from the bucks at this season, when they are mating.'

'What more?' she insisted.

'You need not fear man or boy, woman or child besides, that I do know. No forester will harm another forester. We depend upon one another. Of course there's many an outlaw in hiding, if we did but know precisely where. But they'll mostly keep themselves to themselves. And there's Goody Luke in the great birch wood—she gets called a witch by some. I'd say she's a wise woman, rather . . . Your horse has sense to carry you through boggy places in winter; but on foot watch always for the adder in sunshine.

He was walking barefoot, his hose cut off above the ankle, and he saw her look down and shudder. Then a bird cried, so shrill and harsh and close at hand that she gripped her saddle and hunched her shoulders in fright.

'What's that? What's that?'

Lewis pointed. 'There he goes, look. That's the yaffle. See him? See his green and gold?'

The bird was flying ahead of them, its swooping

convulsive flight drawing scallops in the air. Then it came to a tree and clung to the bark, tapping fast and furiously.

'And his red cap,' cried the girl, childishly pleased with her own observation. 'What did you call him?'

'He's the yaffle. The galleybird. The woodpecker. Take your choice of his names.'

'I'll choose yaffle.' She was smiling now. 'You've a red cap, too,' she said.

He laughed. 'He's made you smile. I began to think you never would. What's your name? I know you're niece to Dame Elizabeth FitzEdmund—but what's your name?'

'I'm Cecily Jolland.' Again she smiled. 'And you're Lewis Mallory. My aunt told me.'

Now they had climbed the steep bank and the weaver's cottage was close at hand. There was no longer any reason or excuse for continuing that way, so Lewis released the bridle and stepped back.

'That's your way, look. I'm going on to the forge. Good day, then, Cecily Jolland; God keep you.'

'And you,' she said, a little patronising. 'And I thank you for your company—Master Yaffle!'

She broke into laughter at that, and pulled at Cressyd's rein; to get quickly away, no doubt, from the dangers of making a joke with a stranger. Lewis watched Cressyd carry her rider briskly over the stream and up to the cottage. The weaver was already at his door, the folded cloth on his arm. Lewis watched for a second or two more, then went on his way. As soon as he got home, he would try to interest his cousin in the idea of selling Zephyr to Dame Elizabeth as a more suitable mount for her niece.

5

The Taste of Freedom

There was a great deal to do before winter set in. At
Ghylls Hatch this meant men's work, but at Mantlemass
orders came from the mistress, and in the shortening days
Dame Elizabeth's household, indoors and out, was occupied for every hour and every minute. The corn off the two
fields had been taken to the miller long ago and now the
sacks of flour stood against the granary walls, with oats
and grains to feed both man and beast in the months
ahead. The pigs which could usually fend for themselves
had still to be catered for in case of snow. The harvest of
acorns was immense, but this was made as far afield as
possible, that the hogs might root near home in fine
weather. It had been a good harvest. There was plenty of

hay, plenty of straw, and vast loads of the cheap litter
harvested off the forest itself, the bracken that sprang
up in June and covered the shallow slopes below the house.
They cut heather, too, for bedding, and re-filled mat-
tresses with straw, for last year's was broken down to
little more than chaff. The old rushes were cleared and
burnt and the floor of the hall freshly strewn. Under the
canopy of the big fireplace there and in the kitchen hams
hung to smoke, and the haunches of venison that were
the perquisites of the manor. There was not the shortage
of meat in winter in this household that troubled many.
The pigeon loft was full, too, and there would be variety
and plenty in the Mantlemass winter fare. Only the stew
pond was giving trouble. It had been newly made a
twelve month before but in the early autumn the fish had
suddenly died and none would live now in the dull water.
Nicholas Forge, who was a knowledgeable man, said the
pond was badly placed. They must dig another, well
away from this one. The sewage from the house, he said,
was dispersed carelessly, and had run into the pond and
poisoned the water. But no one else could make any sense
of this. Didn't they put farmyard muck on the fields to
the advantage of the crop? Then why should a crop of
fish be harmed by human waste?

Cecily had now learned to churn butter, to strip dried
herbs and pound them, to preserve eggs by dipping them
into a solution of beaten whites with gum arabic—a
precious receipt Dame Elizabeth had had years ago from
an old servant in the early days of her marriage. They
would grow a little stale, she admitted, but almost all
would be edible. Dame Elizabeth also spent much time
making a paste of rabbit meat, well spiced and sealed
into jars under a thick layer of lard. Besides all this, there
was the year's brewing standing in the cellar—ale from
hops grown over by the church, much stronger stuff than

the small beer of everyday; wine made from elderberry and cowslip in their season, and nettle beer. There was honey enough this year for a brewing of mead, though this was not always the case, Dame Elizabeth told her niece.

There was a great coney-catch in November. Every Mantlemass tenant came to that, for as the animals were skinned their carcases were given away for meat. Henty sent ferrets into the warrens, and half a dozen dogs were employed. The rabbits poured from the warrens, which had nets covering their opening. Cecily had gone to watch because her aunt was there and had taken for granted that she would go too. But she was unprepared for what took place. The rabbits tumbled and struggled in the nets and the men set about clubbing them. It had to be skilfully done, for the pelts must not be torn by broken bones. With the dogs barking and snarling, the men shouting, many rabbits screaming as they died, the noise was horrible and Cecily had to run away.

Her aunt was pleased with the day's work.

'We build up our stocks during winter, and then the buyers come in spring to collect the skins. I shall show you how to stitch the pelts, Cecily, and between us we might make a cover for your bed.'

'I had fur for my bed in London,' Cecily said. 'I never thought how it was got.'

She had hardly thought at all, it seemed to her by now.

The russet wool gown had been cut and sewn and Cecily was happy to wear it in the increasingly chilly weather. The change in her life was so great that the immediate past began to mist over like last week's dream— though it did not merge with that other dream, older, darker, and lying always a little below her consciousness, waiting to catch her in feverish or half-waking moments.

That riddle remained unsolved, but there were other

riddles that surely could be answered. When she sat
with her aunt in the winter parlour and they stitched the
fur coverlet together, each questioned the other. Dame
Elizabeth sought her answers sometimes boldly, sometimes subtly; and Cecily learnt from her in this as in
other matters.

There was no word of Sir Thomas, no message came,
no rider thundered to the door in pursuit; her father might
as well have died. Sometimes for days Cecily could
hardly remember what he looked like. Nor did she miss
Alys any longer for she had all too clear a notion of how
Alys might behave in these countrified surroundings.

'Why did you say that Alys had sly eyes?' she asked
her aunt as they both sat stitching.

'Sly eyes—sly heart—either will do. She loved you to
your face, but she loved your father more. She was set
to spy upon you and tell your father all you did.'

'I did nothing . . .' Cecily frowned. 'She loved my
father more?'

'And has followed him, if I know women,' Dame
Elizabeth said, stitching fast and angrily. 'And I will
tell you this, niece, now I have told you one thing—
though I am his sister, I am not his loving sister. Once
I was dutiful enough—as a sister is bound to be towards
her brother when their father has died. He made use of
me for his own advancement. When that happened—
then I became his enemy. Do you understand?'

Cecily understood nothing, she was completely bewildered. Only her suspicions of her father's plans and
purposes seemed suddenly to overwhelm her. 'Would he
use me, too, in such a way?' she asked in a low voice.
Trying to vindicate him and comfort herself she added—
'I heard him call me his treasure. . . .'

'And so, indeed, you are. And he will spend his
treasure in his own good time. You have a fortune, Cecily,

from your mother, that your uncle Digby must give up to you when you have your own household.'

'Then,' cried Cecily, for she was still his daughter and he could still command her, 'then if he were so vile as you suggest he would have seen me wed long before now.'

'Matters are not always as simple as they seem, my child. But you need not fear. I have only one purpose in my life—and I have told you of it already. I shall see you happy. Not only for your sake, but for your mother's. The dearest friend any girl could ask for—and I was a girl then. For the sake of three women, Cecily—for your mother, for you, for myself—I shall save you from your father.'

She was bending over her work, her fingers taut, her needle stabbing at the coney skin, and her voice was so low and intense in tone that Cecily began to tremble.

'He will come for me one day, madam.'

'And is that what you wish?'

The girl hesitated, blinking at sudden tears. 'I have already learnt to live differently. Mantlemass is an easier home than my father's . . . Oh,' she cried, bursting out with it, 'I was a poor thing when I lived in London with my father and with Alys!' She remembered the frail hands, the tiny steps, the covered face, the small sighing voice—and she made a sound of complete revulsion. 'Oh what a doll—what a puppet! I was a dead thing—a bundle of sticks tied with gold thread—I was nothing, nothing!'

This outburst completely transformed Dame Elizabeth. She laid down her work, flung back her head and laughed. It was the first time, Cecily realised, that she had heard her aunt laugh quite so loud and free, and it was a good sound—robust and rather coarse, as honest as the farmyard.

'For that truth, my dear niece Cecily, I am ready to bar my door against twenty fathers and all their might!'

At last she was obliged to wipe her eyes, so furiously had the laughter taken her. 'There now,' she said, recovering her breath, 'you have told me everything I needed to know. Truly all daughters, all sisters, are pawns in the game played by their menfolk. Only, Cecily, there was once a move made in this particular game that has not been revoked . . . Now put away the fur and we'll stitch at the tapestry for a change.'

The tapestry was a set of bed hangings, enormous—could it ever reach completion? The design was of a great tree and in every branch there perched birds and butterflies and insects of every kind and colour. Aunt and niece sat together at the big frame, stitching almost in unison, brought together now in a new and stirring companionship.

'How many of the birds can you name for me, Cecily?'

'The thrush, madam. And the ousel. The redbreast—the owl—the swallow. And here's a swan. And a merlin. Oh—and I see one I have only lately learnt. A forest bird—clinging to the tree trunk, you see, as true as life. That is the yaffle,' Cecily said with pride.

'So it is. You are learning. Was it Henty who instructed you? He has a wide knowledge of such things.'

'No,' said Cecily. 'It was the boy with the red cap. We—passed—on the way to the weaver's.' Since her aunt made no exclamation of surprise or disapproval but bent over the tapestry, Cecily let her own pleasure in that meeting carry her to further confidence. 'You told me his name was Lewis Mallory. But because of his red cap I call him Master Yaffle!'

'You have reminded me of something I must do,' Dame Elizabeth said, re-threading her needle. 'I need a load of Master Orlebar's good stone for mending the byre wall. Tomorrow would be as good a day as any other to ride over to Ghylls Hatch. You shall go with me for company.'

The next day was cold, dry and still. Round about noon, Simon the carter brought the horses to the door, Dame Elizabeth's big bay, Farden, and little Cressyd. Cressyd was skittish, and without any thought for meekness or manners Cecily rode her hard up the long slow track to its summit, then turned and walked her back.

'You suit one another well enough,' Dame Elizabeth said, as Cecily settled in at her side. 'But I think you have some of your mother's skill with a horse. Her brothers treated her as one of them and took pride in her. She rode like a boy.'

'My father did say once that I sat my horse well.'

'And for that reason it may be you deserve better than Cressyd. She came from Ghylls Hatch—and so might another.'

'He said—that boy—Lewis Mallory—he said they had a full stable.'

'Horses are Master Orlebar's trade as coneys are mine.'

'Is he an orphan, madam, that he lives here with his cousins?'

'Lewis? Not so. His father is a man of wealth and influence whose eldest son was promised in marriage to a king's daughter, but he died at ten years old. So Lewis should be his father's heir. But he was passed over in favour of the youngest son, and sent away to grow up into a country bumpkin.'

'I thought only daughters were hardly treated. . . .'

'The world is ruled by ambition . . . Do you know that your father married me to a royal bastard? It was a step up the ladder—and why should he care that his sister must suffer a husband with a deformed mind, let alone a warped body. Well—I thank God no child was born alive . . . Look—they're digging a minepit in the wood there,' she said, with no change of tone. 'What a load of trees they've cleared. There won't be a hearth on the forest burning

wood this winter, if so much goes for charcoal. I must tell
Bostel to see we stack more peat.'

The men at work looked up as the two riders passed.
Dame Elizabeth called out a greeting to them, and they
returned it easily. Perhaps it was the hard metal in which
they worked that taught them to be proud, or the knowledge that they traded in life and death—in plough shares
and pitchforks, in swords and arrow heads, in nails and
horseshoes . . . Without iron men would be helpless.

When they came to Ghylls Hatch the jumble of buildings, many of them rather mean, surprised and dis-
appointed Cecily. She had expected another house as
graceful as Mantlemass, but here it was as though the
stables took precedence. Over the acres of grassland the
horses moved all the time.

'He's grazing his animals late,' Dame Elizabeth said.

'There's Lewis Mallory on the black stallion—riding
along by the yard wall. And that's his cousin Orlebar who's
watching.' She made an approving noise. 'The boy's a
handsome rider. There's not much to be taught to either of
them, I daresay, when it comes to horses and their ways.'

It was Lewis who saw the two women approaching.
He wheeled his horse and rode fast towards them, then
pulled up short, so that the horse reared showily.

'We have admired your horsemanship from a distance,
Lewis Mallory,' Dame Elizabeth said dryly. 'Take me to
your cousin. I've business to discuss.' When she had
greeted Roger Orlebar she said at once, 'I'll go into the
house with you. There are two matters to speak about—
stone for a wall, for one.' She touched Cecily's arm briefly,
saying that this was her niece, who had come to be a
daughter to her. 'While we talk, Master Orlebar, let the
boy show her some of your horses.'

This was easy manners. For a second, the gentleman's
daughter Cecily increasingly forgot to be, stiffened her

spine and jerked up her chin. Then pleasure defeated vanity. She said eagerly, 'Yes, pray do that if you will. I should delight in seeing the horses.'

'They are a fairish lot,' Lewis said, dismounting. 'It'd take a week of Sundays to show you all. But I'll show you the best. That's grey Zephyr. She's half-sister to your Cressyd—their dam was a skewbald, chestnut on white. She's a pretty thing, swift and light. A mount for a lady.'

He began walking off as he spoke and she had to run to keep up with him and hear the rest of Zephyr's praises sung. The mare was grazing within a stockade fenced with sturdy posts and rails of split elm. Lewis whistled softly and the creature pricked her ears and looked over her shoulder. Again he whistled, but on a sharper note, and she pawed the ground and tossed her head, then wheeled towards him, long mane and fine tail flying with her easy canter.

'She is an angel of gentleness,' Lewis boasted, when he held her head between his hands. 'Now put your palm against her mouth and feel the softness of it. Have no fear of her, for she will only nuzzle.'

Cecily did as she was bid, and the mare pressed against her palm, blowing with her lips, warmly and gently.

'Oh she is pretty—pretty!' Cecily cried. 'Oh if she were mine! I love Cressyd, but Zephyr is as beautiful as a dream. How far and fast I might ride on her! Where might I ride to?'

'As far as the sea.'

'I never saw it in my life. How should I know the way?'

'Why, I should ride with you,' he replied. 'It would not do to have you lost.'

'And do you know the way?'

'I know all the ways about here,' he boasted.

'Then—when?' she asked, as bold as she was breathless, intoxicated by the freedoms opening up before her, widening and promising. 'When will you show me the sea? When shall we ride—and may it truly be on Zephyr?'

'I have watched you on Cressyd. I know you can handle a spirited horse.'

'I have not ridden so many horses. But sometimes I rode for exercise with my father, and we went over the hills above London. But at the most I have ridden three or four different animals.' She frowned. 'Will you trust me with Zephyr?'

'As I trust Zephyr with you.' He looked up at the sky. 'It should be fine for another day or two. Tomorrow?'

'As far as the sea?'

'Perhaps not to the water's edge—but to the top of the downs, where we may see it all spread before us . . . I will bring out Zephyr and do you bring Cressyd, and where we meet we will change saddles.'

'Where will that be?'

'By the water where we talked?' he suggested. 'Where the pool is.' He grinned. 'Where you called me Yaffle. As good a place as any, since you know it well.'

'Oh yes, I know it very well,' she cried, 'for I have been there since . . .' She had gone there looking for him, and the realisation made her blush. 'I hoped I might see the yaffle again,' she said quickly; but that only made matters worse. 'Of course I must ask my aunt if she will allow me to go with you,' she said, finding a haughty tone of voice.

'Of course, lady,' he said. But he was laughing. They were both laughing, underneath the play of recollected manners. 'When will you be there—supposing Dame Elizabeth consents? It must be early, for the days are short. We shall need to ride hard. You must miss your dinner: are you ready to ride on an empty belly?'

'You talk like a farm boy!'

'Well—how else?' He slapped Zephyr's neck and sent her racing away. 'Country living means country ways.

Before you came to look a country girl I hardly would've dared speak in your ladyship's presence. Or wanted to,' he added rudely. 'Look—your aunt has come from the house and my cousin with her. They are looking for us.'

The sight of Dame Elizabeth alarmed Cecily, for she seemed far more solid and likely to be obstructive than had seemed possible while Lewis was talking of riding hard to the sea. Life had changed, truly, but could it have changed as much as this?

Sir James had come to Ghylls Hatch just as Dame Elizabeth and her niece were leaving.

'Your pupil is bolder than he should be,' Roger Orlebar said to the priest. 'He is set to sell Zephyr to Dame Elizabeth for her niece—and the Dame, God save us, has consented to their riding out together tomorrow. And all she will say to my frowning is that she will send Nicholas Forge with them—if she does not need his services herself.' He shook his head at Lewis. 'This girl is no milkmaid, cousin. You should offer her more respect than to race harum-scarum about the countryside with her.'

'It's great respect to let her ride Zephyr,' Lewis said. 'What a fuss you're in, Cousin Orlebar. I'll see she comes to no harm.'

He had rarely heard such firm talk from his guardian, and he looked hopefully at the priest for support. But Sir James, too, who was a most tolerant man for all his calling, looked unexpectedly solemn. Lewis remembered what Jenufer Orlebar had suggested—that there was some disagreement between the families. But if any such disagreement stemmed from his father he felt little obligation to take on the quarrel as his own.

'Well, it is for Dame Elizabeth to decide the matter,' the priest said at last. 'Perhaps by tomorrow she will have had second thoughts.'

6
Her Mother's Daughter

The thought that Dame Elizabeth might indeed change her mind disturbed the rest of both Lewis and Cecily. Each, waking in the night, experienced the doubts that can come with darkness. The prospect was altogether too easy to seem probable. For Cecily it was the absolute reverse of all she had known, and though so many changes had taken place within her and in her outward circumstances, she could not quite believe that any guardian of any girl of her age would be so free of convention. For she had actually said, as they rode home, 'I must deprive you of Nicholas Forge, my child—I have a document I want him to draw for me.' Lewis knew nothing of that, and by morning had gloomily concluded that the secretary would ride with them, even if they were finally permitted to go at all.

But when he reached the meeting place, riding beneath the dawn sky, Cecily was ahead of him.

'Well,' he said. And then said no more for he had to laugh with pleasure at the sight of her. She was wearing a dark hood that tied under the chin, and the bloodless look which he had noticed when he first saw her standing beside her aunt had given way to a subtle glow of health and good humour.

'Change saddles,' she said. 'I cannot wait to be mounted on Zephyr.' She added primly, 'My aunt regrets, but Nicholas Forge is busy today.'

'Unfortunate,' he murmured. 'For him. But the lady knows me well and knows I am to be trusted. And I take her confidence very kindly.'

'Shall we see the palace?' she asked as she settled into her saddle and watched him mount a rather surprised Cressyd.

'Not today. It is behind us. We must ride hard if we are to return before dark.' He was fiddling with his girths and did not look at her as he said, 'Did you speak to Dame Elizabeth of where we were to ride? How long we might be?'

'I could not say how long if I did not know,' said Cecily. She flushed slightly. She had hurried from the house at the last, terrified that her aunt would call her back, that the whole thing had been a silly joke . . . But Dame Elizabeth said nothing and Cecily had fled unchecked.

'Have you brought food?'

'I have four honey cakes and two apples.'

'You'll starve on that. Just as well I took meat and bread enough for two.'

'How far till we see the sea?'

'Sixteen—seventeen miles, some such.' He straightened

in the saddle at last, caressing Cressyd, who was restive
at the change of weight. 'Are you ready to go? We have a
very fair day for the ride.'

'Yes. Yes, I am ready.'

As she followed after him she was half sick with excitement. How long since she had pursed up her mouth at
riding without an attendant? How long since she had
covered her face before strangers, lowered her eyes before
her father, trembled at the thought of taking a step alone?
She recalled what Dame Elizabeth had told her of her
mother. For her, freedom had come first, then bondage.
But Cecily had been bound and was now free. It was as
though everything in her sight had been shrouded and
small and grey—and now gushed big and full of colour.
There was a threat in all this, but she would not think of
it today: to return to bondage would surely be to die . . .
She would think only that her aunt had promised happiness.

They cantered up the long track from the river below
Mantlemass and the forest opened out in heathland bared
to the wind. Ahead of them rolled more wooded slopes,
but already the thoughts of both strained onward to those
further hills from which they would see the sea.

Lewis touched Cressyd with his heel and she flew into
a gallop. Without any urging, Zephyr followed. The wind
was keen on this upland and the speed of their passing
increased it a hundredfold, so that Cecily's hair streamed
out behind her as bravely as Zephyr's splendid tail, and
her hood began to slip back and back until her head was
bare. The chill air bit at her temples and made her gasp.
Lewis, glancing back at her, saw that she was smiling
widely. Then the woods were ahead and he pulled in
Cressyd gently and easily. Zephyr fretted a bit and
tossed her head, but Cecily held her without difficulty
until she had dropped to a walk.

Lewis shouted over his shoulder, 'You have her well in hand. She is a bird on the wing! Have you ever flown so fast and far before?'

'Never! Never!' *My pretty bird*, her mother had said....

The track here was narrow. They walked singly through the trees that were at last bare of leaf. Out of the wind the pale sun was warm, the sky so high and open it was almost colourless.

'Look there,' said Lewis, checking his horse and pointing down into the valley. 'That's where John Urry made his big hammer.'

'It's quiet.'

'There's been no rain for weeks. There's not enough water to drive it—nor ever will be just there, so Sir James says. He must get himself a better flow or give up. He's a man too sensible to be clever, as they say in these parts. His neighbours are laughing. Old people never want to change,' Lewis said angrily. 'They'll go on and on in the same ways—what was good enough for their fathers is sure to be good enough for them. But that's no way to live. I pray Master Urry will take his plans to a better site and show them all he's got more sense than they have.'

'Will he make swords and lances?'

'He'd like that—but he's the furnace man, not the smith. Still, such things are important. When the king last went to war with France it made a goodly trade for this countryside. Sir James told me this. Arrow heads and bolts for cross-bows. Do you know about the old battles—Agincourt? Crécy? There's pounds of Sussex iron in France by now. Do you know about this?'

'From ballads,' she said, ashamed of her ignorance but proud of him now for knowing so much.

'Sir James could tell you the whole of history. Oh he is full of tales—I could not have a better teacher . . . Now we turn due south. We must drop down to flat ground before we work up again to the downs. Is all well with you, lady?'

'Yes, sir,' said Cecily. She pulled her hood on and settled it firmly, smiling because he was smiling. And she felt the strangeness in the lives of both of them—both newcomers to their surroundings yet becoming native by the very effort of learning new ways and almost a new tongue. Now Lewis was moving off again, and she followed after. They set off briskly through a scattering of trees, then out of them again on to heathland. The village was on their right hand, with the market town ahead, but they cut off behind it and came to flat ground where they picked up a broad road. Lewis shouted over his shoulder that it had been made by the Romans. It stretched ahead as far as Cecily could see, and the horses broke into a canter that did not flag for miles.

Now they came suddenly in sight of the downs, which had crept near without any warning foothills. They reared up out of the plain unlike anything Cecily had seen or imagined. Coming from London to Mantlemass it had been necessary to cross a ridge of hills, but not like these, whose sides seemed shaven to the neatness of moss, whose treeless horizons swooped and scooped against the sky.

The broad road turned a little west, then south, and from the head of a gentle incline it was possible to see a fair town with a castle set above it like a crown. The road ended where the town began.

'Now we must take a marshy way by the river for a while,' Lewis said. 'You can look across the valley and see St Pancras Priory below the town. It is all of four hundred years old. At least—'

'—that is what Sir James says,' Cecily finished for him.

'Mock, if you must,' he said airily. 'I'd be an ignorant clod without him.'

It was noon as they rode a slippery chalk track up the side of the downs.

'Are we almost there?' Cecily called.

'Almost. Give me the bridle and I shall lead Zephyr. And you, Cecily Jolland, close your eyes till I command you to open them.'

She laughed, winding her hands in Zephyr's mane when the reins were taken from her, and closing her eyes tightly. She swayed giddily and cried out as the horse was led onward, and clutched wildly at the saddle.

'You dare not open your eyes!' he cried. 'Do so—and I swear to see you never ride Zephyr again!' He seemed to be leading her on and upward interminably, but at last he reined in and the horses stood still, their sides heaving. 'Now,' he said. 'Open your eyes.'

They were higher than she had expected. Ahead, the cropped turf dropped away, and beyond and above the wintery green the great expanse of the ocean stretched for ever against the sky. Sprinkled with the glitter of the winter sunshine, the sea which Cecily had only imagined or seen pictured, was less silver than pewter, and on the metal there winked and shimmered and shifted and slithered what looked like innumerable coins, or the scales of uncountable thousands of leaping fish.

'Oh God save us all!' she cried. 'What a wonder!'

'It is France on the far side,' he told her. 'You cannot see it, but it is there. Do you know why this is so?' He looked over his shoulder, as though there might be someone lurking in that quiet place—the shepherd say, who must be somewhere near, for his flock was moving over the brow. 'Sir James believes it to be because the world is as round as an orange. But never breathe it to anyone. It could be called blasphemy.'

She had never heard such nonsense and she burst out laughing. 'If I am standing here on an orange,' she cried, 'you had better hold me lest I fall off!'

'Look around you, lady,' he said, fierce and despising her foolishness. 'What do you see but a clean line of the sky that does not end? It is a circle round us. As though we stand on a platter.' He added, with some pride, 'Sir James thought of the orange, but the platter is my idea.'

'And when we come to the edge of the platter—we tumble over into France?' She was helpless with laughter.

'I should have known better than to tell you. Women have not the wit to understand such matters.'

He was looking very stern, his eyebrows drawn darkly together. He had fine eyes, full of fire and purpose, and his nostrils were drawn back scornfully. She found herself, checked in her laughter, studying his face with eyes that had not until now been properly opened. He was handsome, proud, noble, brave . . . The words streamed through her head and she was startled by their vehemence. She had looked at him with pleasure from the start, but now she truly saw him. What she saw seemed the best that life had ever shown her. In this keen intelligent face, the mouth already firm but kind, she knew without any doubt at all she was seeing all the future that she would ever desire. Tears rushed to her eyes, tears of promise, of hope, of anxiety and dread of loss . . . He was too busy with his platter and his orange to notice her silence.

'Sir James himself shall instruct you,' he declared.

'Yaffle! Yaffle!' she mocked, her voice high and excited. 'That's a true name for you—for there you go, boring away into mysteries as though they were tree trunks! Mind what you say and who you say it to, Master Yaffle. Any one of us may be charged with blasphemy!'

'Then it must be you who testifies against me,' he retorted, 'for none else has been given the chance.'

6

'Is this a quarrel?' she asked, not minding, for she knew it would be made up.

'No, it is *not* a quarrel!' His frown eased out. He began to grin. 'It's hours past dinner time. Shall we eat here, before we turn back?'

'Let us wait until we reach the sea.'

'That's another league, I'd say. The dark will catch us long before we're home.'

'I want to see how it looks where it meets the earth. Are there great waves? Take me to see, Lewis. I'll ride as hard as a messenger all the way home.'

'Your aunt will be angry—'

Cecily prodded Zephyr and shot past Cressyd, making for the long shallow track that ran along the side of the hill and at last flattened out into the valley that became the river's mouth. She heard Cressyd thundering behind her —if Cressyd with her light swift gait could ever be said to thunder. Lewis was edging up to overtake Zephyr, but the track was not wide enough and he was obliged to drop back again. Cecily looked over her shoulder. She was breathless with laughing as she had never laughed before, with riding as she had never ridden before. Lewis defeated her by stepping his horse off the track, taking a lower scoop and coming up a hundred yards ahead of her. Zephyr was the swifter horse, but Cressyd's rider was the more experienced horseman. They checked, as winded as the horses. Here the track steepened and they had to pick their way. Suddenly they were at the foot of the hills, riding sedately by a hamlet with a church that stared along the river's back to the sea.

This was marshy land and they crossed it along an ancient causeway. Reeds on either side rattled their winter bones, and on a smaller, lighter note the seeds of sea-poppy chattered in brittle pods. Close by the shore which stretched on either hand to chalky cliffs, a mill stood whose great wheels were turned by the ebb and flow of the tide. Where the fields met the shingle Lewis dismounted and gave his hand to Cecily. They led the horses along the high bank, watched by the miller, his blank-faced wife and half a dozen tousled children.

'Look there!' Cecily cried, as Lewis tied the horses to a willow stump. 'There it is! The great ocean and the waves breaking!' She darted forward, but the shingle shifting under her feet threw her to the ground. Lewis pulled her up and they struggled over the beach together. The waves were small in the quiet winter sunshine, breaking in pearly bubbles along the edge of the stones. 'Oh—if I had never seen such a thing!' she cried. 'That I might have died without knowing! Should we let the horses drink?'

He gave a shout of laughter. 'You are the most ignorant creature I ever did see, Cecily Jolland. It's salt! It's salt as tears! Did no one ever tell you?'

'Why should they?' she demanded. 'And why would I care—until I saw it?' She crouched down and dipped her fingers in the cold water and tasted them—then sprang back shrieking as the sea ran trickling over her shoes.

Presently they came to a place where shingle had mounded on three sides of a hollow. Lewis shook out the cloak he had carried rolled on his saddle and spread it on the fine stones. He bowed Cecily to a seat and then crouched down and began to unwrap the cloth that held meat and bread and a wedge of goatsmilk cheese. Cecily in her turn took from her pocket the honey cakes and the apples. The cakes were sadly flattened.

'Those make a poor show,' Lewis complained. 'You could have done better than that. Anyone knows that Dame Elizabeth keeps a good larder. My cousin Orlebar has only his sister Jenufer to care for his household. And she's a sad sort of manager. A bit *dunch* as they say. The servants mock her and the place is dirty often as not.'

'Why do you live there?' asked Cecily.

For a second he did not reply. The bold question had taken him by surprise.

'Why should I not?' he said at last.

'That's another question. The first deserves a better answer.'

'I am there by my father's wish,' he said, busy with the food, dividing it neatly—but deciding that he needed more than she did because he was bigger, older, stronger and a man.

'As I am at Mantlemass.'

'Partly so.'

'Why—how is different for you?'

He sat back on his heels and said very calmly and coldly, 'Your father has not disowned you, I think.'

'I was a hindrance to him. He left me with my aunt because it suited him, though he despises her.' She was trembling as she said this, and she added boldly and bitterly, 'He did it for his own safety. Nothing else would have persuaded him to leave me at Mantlemass.'

'You are in good hands.'

'I never wish to live with my father again,' she cried, excited beyond sense by the confidence she felt in Lewis Mallory, and in herself. 'My aunt will not make me return.'

'But he can make you, if he wants,' said Lewis sombrely. 'Fathers do as they wish with their children. They break their hearts if it suits them, as easily as they would wring a chicken's neck to make a meal!'

Cecily was silent. She would not be shaken. For her it was to be different. There was a mystery and the mystery would save her. Her aunt had said: *There was a move made in this particular game that has not been revoked.* Though the words were without any sense, yet they were a reassurance. They suggested a locked door whose key had been thrown away; before the door could be opened, the key must be recovered. . . .

'My father had three sons,' said Lewis, handing Cecily bread and meat. 'It is like a ballad. But I am only the second son. It is always the youngest who is the hero.'

"Now the next verse. . . ?'

'I know that I was once dearly loved. I cannot recall anything I did to lose that love. But I think of it as little as possible. It is over now and I am settled. It is far better to forget.' But because she was waiting and listening he was obliged to continue. 'When I was seven years old the king went into France, all of us and my father with him. The eldest son, my brother Geoffrey, rode into battle as his page. He was ten years old and he died with an arrow in his throat.'

Cecily bit her lip and was silent.

'So then I was my father's heir, and made much of. I turned eight that year, and I remember being taken to court, and to many other fine places. To France, and once even further—perhaps to Rome, but I cannot remember. One thing I do recall—it is that King Edward gave me a sword that was three times the length of my own arm!' He frowned, tossing a handful of pebbles up and down, so that they scraped and scratched together monotonously. 'I wonder who has it now. It was taken away with all the rest.'

'What could you have done to deserve it?'

'If I knew that . . . Well, what does it signify now? I have my own life and I know it is a good one.'

'Was it long ago that you came to Ghylls Hatch?' Cecily asked, for he had told her too little and she had to prod him on to further confidence. 'How old were you then?'

'I was ten. Geoffrey was ten when he died—perhaps my father could not bear to see me in his place . . . All I

know now is that my father one day was in a high rage.
How it started—that I can't remember. I only have a
memory of his roaring fury and the noise in the great hall,
and my mother weeping and shrieking and my old nurse
with her . . . And I remember riding on a rainy day to my
cousins—not Orlebar, but some others I forget now, in a
country place north of London. But I was only there a
short while—some months, perhaps—and just growing
used to the change, when my father came roaring after
me yet again, and brought me in a day's journey to Ghylls
Hatch. And I have never seen nor heard of him since.
He would not know me, I daresay, nor I him. For he
will have grown old and I have become a country lad.'

'Fathers are indeed beyond comprehension,' Cecily
said.

'So you see,' Lewis said, smiling at her rather wanly,
'the youngest son was the hero, for he became my father's
heir in my place.' He moved restlessly. 'You must eat.
Surely you are hungry? I am.'

They sat for a while in silence, then Cecily asked the
question she needed to ask, whose answer she dreaded.
'What shall you do, now that you are grown?'

He stopped munching and looked at her, his face
bulging and comical. When he had swallowed he said,
'What would you have me do?'

'You must answer.'

'I am man enough to fight and die. Shall I go to be a
soldier? There are always battles.'

'But you are only the second son,' she reminded him.
'The first son is the warrior; the second may be a scholar.'

'A scholar . . . A cleric? You mean I should enter the
church?' he asked, frowning.

'I cannot see you a cardinal, Master Yaffle—and none
else in the church wears a red cap!'

'Finish your meat,' he said, trying not to laugh. 'What

shall I do now? No doubt I shall stay as I am. For it is not so bad to be a countryman, Cecily Jolland. The priest will teach me all he knows of scholarship, and if I remember one quarter of it I shall be a learned fellow. Horses and books are as good company as any man could wish. Though they say ladies prefer a hero.'

'A dead hero—or a live scholar . . . I know which I would choose,' cried Cecily. And then corrected herself, 'I know which I would choose to be.'

It was warm in the hollow out of the wind, where the sun shone unclouded. The waves pulled on the shingle in a rhythm Cecily had never heard before. Then the miller's children came to stand and stare, very close and gazing piercingly at the food the two were eating.

'Shall I give them the cakes, Lewis?'

'I am still hungry!'

'They are hungrier. What little scarecrows—and thin as last year's bolster! Here!' She held out the cakes and the children shifted nearer; but like birds afraid to venture the last yard for a crumb, they kept darting back and hiding one behind the other.

'It is more than time we turned for home,' Lewis said. 'Leave the cakes on the stones. Lord—what a stench!' he added, pinching his nose. 'The farmyard's like lavender and roses to this collection of young animals.'

It was a steep pull up out of the hollow, the shingle shifting and falling around their feet. Lewis gave Cecily his hand and pulled her up to the ridge, and kept her hand in his until they reached the horses. Behind them the children pounced on the four cakes that must be divided among six, and their cries of fury were far harsher than the cries of the gulls which swooped above them.

'At least you and I have never starved,' said Lewis soberly. 'You asked what I should do with my life, but

what will you do, Cecily Jolland, if your father does not
send for you?'

'I shall live at Mantlemass.'

'Yet you hated it when you came.'

'I was another person. I was a dead thing—I was
nothing—nothing!' cried Cecily, clinging now to his hand
with both her own and speaking so wildly and fiercely
that he was dismayed.

'Well, you are not a dead thing any more,' he said, in
the gentle voice he would use to a frightened horse.

'But now I know—I know it quite clearly and suddenly
—I know I should die if I had to go back.'

'You have told me your aunt would not let you go.'

'What if something should happen to her—if she should
take sick and die—?'

'All this death and despair . . . Your eyes are full of
tears!'

'But what should I do without her?'

'You have other friends. You have Orlebar and
Mallory.' He urged her to her horse. 'We must ride home.
We have stayed far too long. And we have come too far,
as well. We have only two hours of good daylight.'

'It was my fault. I will tell my aunt so.'

'You are not to weep for what may never happen,' he
said seriously, as he helped her to mount.

'I am better. Forgive me.'

'Follow me closely, then. We must not waste any time.'

He led off and she followed obediently. Already the
sun was leaning well down the sky and they had a long
way to go. They rode at an easy canter, and in silence.
Sometimes Lewis looked round to see that all was well
with Zephyr and her rider, but he did not pause until
they were breasting the downs. The forest lay ahead of
them, the dusk already gathered to its steeper slopes.
In these last hours the sky had subtly changed. The wind

had dropped, the cold had increased. There was a hint of saffron in the sky, and along the horizon clouds curled like heavy plumes of grey and purple.

Lewis dropped to a trot and they rode side by side until they came to the road. 'There's snow to come,' Lewis said. 'This side of January it need not be severe. It is after Christmas that the trouble comes. Then, if there are drifts, it is all but impossible to move about the forest. We are mewed up under our own roofs until the thaw.' He looked at Cecily through the growing dark. 'Is all well with you again? Are you ready to ride hard the rest of the way?'

'Yes. I am ready.' She looked pale and tired but she was bound to obey him. It was her fault they were late, she insisted, but he knew he should not have given in to her desire to reach the shore.

There was still some light in the sky when they came near Mantlemass and the spot where they had met that morning. But Lewis would not consider parting here at this time of the evening. None the less, he did halt and wait for her, for he thought he had found a means to reassure her. It was true enough that some ill might befall her aunt, and then indeed she might need friends to help her.

'Before we part—let me say what is in my mind.' He moved up close. He put his hand to his throat and pulled out the ring he wore hidden under his shirt. 'This is my talisman,' he told her. 'Give me your hand.'

Cecily expected to feel some holy medallion in her hand, but what he gave her was a heavy ring. When she had grasped it he closed his hand over hers.

'This is to pledge my friendship and my duty,' he said solemnly. 'What I vow on this ring, which is all I have to prove I am my father's son, I must in honour perform. So I vow to you, Cecily Jolland, that I shall strive to see

you content and safe in that way of life you shall choose.
And if any disaster should come to your aunt, then I
will take up her task, and I will stand between you and
whatever you detest. Even your own father and even in the
face of death . . . Amen. And you—you also say Amen.'

'Amen,' said Cecily, her voice light and breathless.

'Hurry, now,' he said.

But she still held the ring, and in doing so she held the
wearer tethered. 'Let me see it,' she said.

'There's not light enough. I'll show it another day. It is
not known that I wear it,' he told her warningly. 'So do
not speak of it.'

She opened her hand, then, releasing him, and they
moved off at once. They reached the door of Mantlemass
just as lights were being carried to the hall. Dame
Elizabeth wearing a cloak against the cold evening, was
crossing the courtyard from the farm. Cecily shrank a
little when she saw her, as if she could not hope for
anything but anger. But there was no anger to come.

'How far did you take her, Lewis? I looked for you
two hours ago.'

'Madam, we did ride far, indeed. I should have known
better. To the seashore, no less.'

'God save us,' she said, laughing, 'it was not a lazy day
you chose. You have never seen the ocean, niece.'

'No, madam. And how strange it is, and how beautiful.'
Her mind was filled with the pledge Lewis had made to
her and her voice sounded far away in her own ears.
'And Zephyr,' she managed, 'is like a creature from a
dream.'

'Then we will ask Master Orlebar if he will part with
her.'

'He will part with her to this rider, madam,' Lewis
said, 'but to none other!'

'We'll speak of it very shortly—tell your cousin . . . I

have come from the byre. One of the cows is sick and
may very well die. That's a poor start to the winter . . .
Come in now, Cecily. Goodnight to you, Lewis Mallory.'

'Goodnight, madam,' Lewis said, bowing. He bowed,
also, to Cecily. 'And to you, lady. God rest you both.'

Indoors, out of the biting cold and standing by the
bright burning logs in the winter parlour, Cecily was so
struck with fatigue that she sank down by the hearth and
felt she would never move again.

'You rode too far,' Dame Elizabeth said. 'But I see you
are your mother's daughter after all, and that pleases me.'

'I was afraid you would be angry.'

'Angry? Why should I be? I have known young Mallory
long enough to trust him—even with you, my dearest
Cecily.'

Fatigued as she was, Cecily still felt vaguely puzzled by
her aunt's easy ways.

'He told me about his father,' she said, fighting a
yawn, 'and how he is disowned.'

'Did he? What did he say? Did he tell you why his
father treated him in this fashion?'

'He cannot tell at all. Do you know, madam?'

'How should I?'

'You know so much . . . ' This time the words almost
smothered themselves as the yawn defeated her. 'What is
the Mallory crest, madam?'

'A lark within a chaplet of laurel, and a laurel leaf in its
mouth.'

The heat from the fire was suddenly so great that
Cecily was dizzy and almost fainting. She tried to recover
herself, hearing her aunt's voice echoing and repeating
endlessly: *A lark within a chaplet of laurel and a laurel
leaf in its mouth* . . . She struggled against the words for
already they were leading her into that strange half-
conscious dreaming which both lured and frightened her.

She sank into the confusion of familiar images—she saw the winking jewel in the ear of the dark-bearded man, the purple of his grey-bearded elder, the shy boy. *My bird— my poor bird* . . . came the voice she knew to be her mother's.

As she struggled back she saw the emblem of the bird carrying something in its beak, and she named it triumphantly. It was the lark and the laurel of the Mallory crest. She was sure of it, even though she had not seen the ring that hung hidden round Lewis Mallory's neck. Everything seemed quite clear to her, then. Her dream, if dream it was to be called, was not as she had all this time supposed a memory of the past—but a prediction of the future. As Cecily opened her eyes on this conviction, it was as though she and Lewis were already promised to one another.

7
Snowfall to Christmas

During the night the snow began. Lewis woke and slid under the bed covers, the room was so cold. If this had happened yesterday there could have been no ride to the coast, no confidences, no solemn promise. He had assured Cecily that early snow never stayed long, but he remembered now that in the first winter of his being at Ghylls Hatch the snow came on the twentieth day of November, and that same snow was still there, buried under many feet more, when March brought a thaw. If that should happen this year it could mean that Ghylls Hatch and Mantlemass would be quite cut off from one another. The thought made Lewis groan. But if the snow was severe enough to keep him from seeing Cecily, it would also keep her

father away. That at least was a more comfortable
thought. He was glad when morning came. He went out
with a lantern to see what was happening. The forest was
only thinly covered, but the snow was still falling. Lewis
went at once to the stables. There would be a heavy day's
work to get through, for there was not a full winter's stock
of litter and feed in the lofts. He called as he went for the
boys, Peter and Timothy, who worked with the horses.

Peter came running from Zephyr's stall. He had just
tumbled down the ladder from the loft where he slept,
and his hair was full of straw.

'Sir, there's no Timothy. He never come to his bed. I
woke up dunnamany times and looked across for him.'

'What's he about, then?'

'Gone, I reckon. Gone.' Peter looked at Lewis as though
he was too scared to say any more, but then the words
burst from him. 'He's taken Zephyr with him!'

As the snow continued the animals grazing free in the
forest had begun to move in towards home for shelter.
At Mantlemass there was a scurrying of men and maids
about last minute tasks. The sick cow had died in the
night and had to be buried in hard ground. Henty brought
more coney pelts to be stacked within the house, to be
worked during the winter. Wood and peat was carted
indoors.

Before dinner time, Cecily found a small boy crying
in the hall. She knew him vaguely. He was the son of a girl
who worked in the kitchen.

'Why are you here, Davy?' she asked him. 'And what
are you crying for? Where's your mother? Where's
Joan?'

At this he broke out into terrible bawling, sobbing and
shaking and smearing his dirty face with his filthy hands.
He could not speak a word—not indeed that he ever

managed more than two at a time, though he was easily
four years old.

'Come with me to the kitchen,' Cecily said. 'We'll find
your mother.'

She was chary of the mission, for she had twice tried
to speak to the boy's mother and been shamefully
intimidated by Joan's bitter, mocking manner and the
harshness with which she treated the child. Moll Thomsett, who had charge of the household cooking, in her
turn shouted and struck at Joan; so that the Mantlemass
kitchen could not be said to invite visitors. Agnes Bunce
from the dairy was working with Moll when Cecily
appeared, with Davy close behind her skirt.

'Where's Joan, Moll?' asked Cecily, trying to imitate
her aunt's commanding manner.

'Well may you ask it! Gone from here and left her brat
behind her. Gone with that Timothy that works with the
horses at Ghylls Hatch—that's what Agnes say.'

'He come last night,' said Agnes, 'and Joan was off
pillion. He stole the horse, most like.'

'Be hanged if they catch him,' shouted Moll Thomsett.
'The slummocky villain!'

'Is it really true?' cried Cecily, horrified. 'You mean she
has left the boy?'

'What would you suppose? The sooner he goes after
her, the better for all. There's no place under any decent
roof for his kind. Let him get on his ways.'

'He's a baby, Moll. Where would he go?'

'Back to the swank where his mother bore him. Where
else?'

'I don't know what *swank* means . . . '

'Means boggy,' murmured Agnes. 'They do say she
had him down the hollow—it's rare swanky thereabouts.'

'You are abominable! Both of you! My aunt shall hear
of your talk.' Cecily swung round to leave the kitchen. If

need be, she would look after the child herself. 'Where is he?' she cried. 'Where's he gone?'

Moll Thomsett laughed, turning back to the fire, but Agnes, younger and kinder, said quickly, 'He'll not be far, lady. I'll find him.'

'Stay where you are and mind your work!' snapped Cecily.

She ran from the kitchen and across the hall, calling the child's name. There was no sign of him; but when she went to the door she saw his tracks in the snow, rapidly filling as the fall continued. Without stopping for thought, she ran out into the lightly falling flakes. The snow spun aimlessly, spiralling through the quiet air that seemed quite warm, for there was no breath of wind. Almost at once the boy's footprints were covered and she lost the track. She stood calling and calling, so that the carter, hearing the distress in her voice, paused in his work and asked what was wrong.

'Sim—have you seen Joan's Davy? Did he run this way?'

'A minute past. Going home, I thought. But Joan's not there—'

'I know that!'

Cecily turned and ran. The snow was in her hair and on her shoulders, but she could not stop. She picked her way to the hovel where Joan had lived with her boy— one room and a chimney, a beaten earth floor and a bed of rags and sacking. The place was empty, but she picked up his track again and followed it down the slippery hillside below the farm. The rapidly filling prints ended at a tangle of gorse and bramble which made a shelter against the weather; the child had crept inside. He was crouching there with his knees drawn up to his chin, his eyes black and enormous in a face smeared with tears and dirt, his teeth chattering where they met—for he had lost the bottom two.

'Davy, Davy,' wheedled Cecily. 'You must come home out of the snow. Give me your hand and I will help you.' The snow was becoming troublesome, dragging at her skirt and piling and clinging in her hair. She tried to pull the boy out of his hiding place, but he fought her, hard and silently, until she lost her temper out of sheer annoyance and discomfort. 'Do as I bid you!' she cried.

It was what he was used to, and he crawled out at once, looking terrified. Before she came to Mantlemass she would have thought such a child far removed from her interest. But now she clasped him against her skirt, brushing off the snow and pulling a fold of the stuff round him. She began to struggle up the track with him, slipping and slithering and almost falling. She had not gone more than a few paces when she heard a shout behind her. A black horse appeared from behind the thickening veil of falling white. It was Ebony, with Lewis Mallory in the saddle.

'Are you out of your wits?' he called. 'The snow's all over you. You have white hair, Cecily Jolland.'

'I had to find this child. His mother's left him. Joan from the kitchen's his mother.'

'Joan?' cried Lewis. 'I know all about her. And I know who's gone with her.' He swung out of the saddle and began to beat the snow from Cecily's shoulders and hair. He took off his cloak and wrapped it round her. 'If you want to keep the boy warm you must take him before you. And that means you must ride astride as your great grand-dam would have done.' Without asking any permission he took her round the waist and hoisted her into the saddle, then swung Davy up in front of her, tucking the cloak round him. 'It's my stable boy, Timothy, that's gone with her,' Lewis said. 'And it's Zephyr they've ridden away on.'

'Oh not Zephyr!' she cried. 'Not my Zephyr!'

7

'Farewell to your lovely mount, my lady.'

As he led Ebony towards the house the snow fell on his red cap and almost covered it. Cecily was abashed by her situation, for it did seem the height of barbarity and immodesty to find herself with a foot in either stirrup and her skirts rucked up to her calves. Yet for all that she felt safe and sturdy, and the warmth that had glowed in her from the moment she heard Lewis's voice must surely be enough to thaw a mountain of snow and ice. The loss of Zephyr was almost nothing to her now. She had more important matters to dream about.

'Let me down here,' she called, as they came near the house. 'I'll swear my aunt has ridden like a man in her day, but I won't have the servants jeering. Let me down, Master Yaffle.'

Lewis lifted her down, but then held her by the elbows for a second. 'This is a fierce snow. Maybe the winter will be a hard one.' He looked down at her, smiling slightly. 'If we are all mewed up, remember me till spring.'

He released her and turned at once to re-mount.

'Your cloak!'

'Keep it till you are in shelter. I'll come for it when the weather clears.'

The moment he was in the saddle he wheeled Ebony and spurred off, and the snow swallowed him on the instant, as if it were fog. . . .

Dame Elizabeth was angry with Joan and full of grumbles about Davy. He would have to go to his grandmother, who lived somewhere about the forest.

'I will care for him,' Cecily said. 'He shall make no trouble for another living soul.'

'You will tire of that, niece . . . And do you mean to keep him in the house?' demanded Dame Elizabeth, as if Cecily had begged to introduce a piglet or a lamb. 'For if so, he must be cleaned.'

'Yes, I will clean him,' Cecily agreed, eyeing Davy's matted hair and feeling her fingers curl slightly. 'In a year or two, madam, he will make a splendid little page.'

Her aunt laughed at that, saying her niece was growing shrewd; but no more was said about sending the child away.

'Now you have me to care for you,' Cecily told him, as he sat looking over the folds of Lewis's cloak like a black-eyed goblin. But she was not too sure that he understood, or, if he did, whether he fancied the arrangement.

Cecily called Mary Butterfield and Meg. Mary was too fastidious to touch the child, but Meg, a compassionate girl, entered readily into the business of cleaning him up. She soon filled a tub with warm water. Davy, rigid and screaming, bore it only because there was no escape. Meg held him firmly and Cecily scrubbed, her sleeves rolled up, her face red with exertion. Once Moll Thomsett came from the kitchen and stood in the doorway to watch; but she said nothing, and presently went away.

'We must guard him from Moll,' Cecily told Meg.

'She's got a swingeing tongue, truly. I seen her swork and I hear her sworle—'

'*Swork*, Meg? *Sworle*?'

'Well, that's plain enough, surely,' Meg protested. 'It mean she get angered and snarly like a dog.'

'We must cut his hair off and burn it.'

'Sweal it, shall we?'

'Oh *Meg*—how am I to know what you mean? Fetch me a shears!'

'Sweal's what you do with a taper to clean a pig's hide,' Meg explained. 'Still—the pig's dead.'

By now Davy had stopped screaming and merely sobbed. Cecily clipped his hair short as a monk's, then ducked him back into the water and washed his head with such vigour that Meg put in a word for him.

'Mind he don't fall faint and swimey, the way you were taken last evening, lady!' She was laughing and Cecily laughed, too.

Cecily was happy. She was learning companionship. She and Meg were at this moment far indeed from the mistress and servant relationship that Cecily had known with Alys. They were merely two girls of an age, employed on a task that was bound to make them laugh. Now Davy was clean, and the effort and the grief of it all had made him drowsy. He leant more and more against Cecily, and at last his eyes closed altogether. She sat by the hearth and he slept against her knee. She would be kinder to him than his mother had been, she told herself; but which of them would seem the better to him?

Meg was kneeling near Cecily, and now she sat back on her heels and looked at the pair.

'When shall you and I be wed, lady, and have our own?' she said in a small soft voice.

'What talk!' cried Cecily, but softly, too, for fear of waking Davy. 'Is there some lad you fancy, Meg?'

'There's Sim Carter's son, John. But he's a bit faddy and looks above him. Still, if all fays well—it might be he'd think of it.' She looked under her lashes at Cecily. 'And you, lady?'

'The country grows many things, but not suitors,' Cecily replied. 'How hot the fire is—I'm quite burning my cheek.'

'But there's none of us needs more than one,' Meg murmured.

'Where shall Davy sleep?' Cecily asked, deciding, though in a friendly way, that Meg was going altogether too far. 'It had best be with me. He shall be my bodyguard and sleep by the door.'

The wind blew from the north for ten days on end, and almost all that time the snow was falling, now fast, now sparely. Each day at Mantlemass the men worked to dig paths between the house and the farm where the animals steamed and stamped. Muck and snow piled up in the byres. Thin, scummy ice covered the pond where the fish would not breed. Now the long preparations, the storing and the brewing and the preserving kept the household at Mantlemass in good heart. There was provision made, her aunt told Cecily, for every day to be snowy from now until the spring. When the wind dropped the sun came out and all day long the sky was blue. The snow melted on the branches, then froze again at night, so that next day in a small breeze branches and twigs tinkled together. Deer came out of the forest and stood in a cluster at the edge of the trees. Henty would gladly have taken a buck for fresh meat, but all were thin and poorly-looking and not worth the effort. Dame Elizabeth thought they should be fed some litter and grain and so fattened for another day. At this Henty, who was no respecter of persons, gave a guffaw out of his big red beard that echoed over the farmland and sent the deer bolting back among the trees.

'Now we have lost them, skin and bone and all,' said Dame Elizabeth. But she sounded indulgent. She never contrived to outface Henty, and perhaps she liked him all the better for it. 'If I had my way,' she insisted, 'we might dine off fresh fat meat at Christmas, housebound or no.'

'There'll be a thaw before then,' he promised her. 'Give it three more frosts and then we'll see.'

'We're a long way from freedom yet.' Dame Elizabeth looked at her niece, who was sitting by the table making six-inch bags out of fine linen to be filled from a great bowl of lavender and rose leaves. 'What do you say, niece?

Should you enjoy a feast at your own board this year, if
the weather is kind? There shall be Master Henty, with
his daughter and his poor son. And Tom Bostel and Anis,
and perhaps their eldest girl. And Nicholas Forge—but
not, save us, his old mother. And all the rest shall come
who serve me about the house. For it is a feast for man
and master alike. Besides, though we have not so many
neighbours—we have some. What do you say, then,
Cecily?'

'What neighbours?' Cecily asked, stitching the linen
so fine she had to bend her head and hide her face to see
what she was up to.

'What neighbours would you choose to see?'

'Master Orlebar seems a good-hearted man,' Cecily
murmured. 'Should he come?'

'Indeed he should come. Likewise his poor sister. And
shall we ask also his cousin?'

'Why, yes—if it pleases you, madam.'

'There's my good, sweet, submissive girl! See how
obedient and long-suffering your father's harshness has
made you. For my sake—you will endure Master Orlebar's
cousin. Bless your sweet temper!'

'But,' said Cecily, crimson in the face, partly at her
aunt's teasing and partly with the effort of checking her
laughter, 'we are in God's hand. For first the snow must
melt—and on the right day.'

'We will all pray for a thaw. And we will ask Sir James,
too, to take a seat at our table. Which should be pleasing
to heaven as well as to us. For he is a fine, good man, with
a very pleasant humour.'

They must have prayed well, for the thaw began on the
last Sunday of Advent, three days before Christmas Eve.
The still forest gushed and streamed. Whatever had been
dry became wet, and now there was more chance of
drowning, so Meg said, than of sliding and falling and

breaking bones. Davy ran down to the water's edge and
poked about with sticks. It was strange to see how he
never went near the place where he had lived with his
mother, but ran in and out of Mantlemass as though it had
always been his home.

Dame Elizabeth sent Nicholas Forge riding to Ghylls
Hatch to ask the Orlebars for their company at noon on
Christmas Day, and from there he was to go in search of
Sir James. Although Cecily was sure in her heart that they
must come, she waited on pins till her aunt's secretary
returned with the answer.

'Sir James was already at Ghylls Hatch,' he told Dame
Elizabeth, 'so my journey was halved. And all thank you
for your courtesy and will be glad to come to Mantlemass
on Christmas Day.'

'There now, Cecily,' said her aunt. 'You and I must set
about ordering the feast.'

While she waited for Nicholas Forge to return from
Ghylls Hatch, Cecily had been adding to the pile of
lavender bags, at which she stitched for some time every
day—Dame Elizabeth had said she needed one hundred.
She counted them—and there were fifty. Her fingers
were sore with stitching. Her hands by now were greatly
changed; what had been so white and tender had hardened and darkened. What would Alys say if she could
see them? And what, in heaven's name, would her father
think of the coming feast, the freedom and the assorted
company with whom she would happily sit down? Since
the moment when she had seemed to see her own future,
when the lark and the laurel swam out of dream into
reality, Cecily had banished all thought of her father.
Now she experienced a sharp spasm of fear, and if Lewis
had been there she would have cried out to him for help
as she had done as they walked together by the shore.
She still had a father. Unless he died, she was bound

to see him again. Where was he? And was Alys with him? And what plans were they making, far away in France, that even now might come between her and what she most desired?

In the flurry of preparing the feast, even Moll Thomsett grew a shade more mellow, though she had chilblains and the worst was on her nose. But the planning and the counting, the baking and boiling and roasting pleased her sense of self importance. The feast would not happen save for Moll being there, and the knowledge gave her great pleasure and puffed up her pride.

The weather stayed warmish and damp. At night the stars shone mistily, the moon floated through a cloud. Early on Christmas morning they rode through the dark to the church three miles away. They made a fine cavalcade—Dame Elizabeth and Cecily, Henty and the Bostels and Nicholas Forge. Henty's daughter rode pillion, Nicholas Forge took Mary Butterwick, and since Anis Bostel had her own mount, her husband Tom took Meg behind him. The rest of the household had to make do with whatever devotions they could manage for themselves.

The church was cold and in poor repair, damp peeling the coloured paint from the walls and tarnishing the gold ornamentation. The priest, too, was very old and tired, and Cecily wished they could have gone to the palace chapel, where Sir James would officiate—and where most certainly Mallory and Orlebar would be kneeling with their own people. Here in the village church the congregation was of a fair size, for men and women alike had ridden or tramped in from the forest and the hamlets to hear mass on this good day of the year. Afterwards, as neighbour greeted neighbour, Cecily stood at her aunt's side in her coney-lined cloak feeling happy and secure.

The day was ahead of her, she had forgotten all her fears.
She felt warm in body and comfortable in spirit and full
of love for God and man. She could hardly wait until they
rode home to Mantlemass and set about the next part of
the day. The wind had gone back to the north and they
rode into it. Henty looked at the sky, only just growing
light, and said that winter would soon be back . . . .

The guests rode in precisely at noon. Cecily was still
struggling to change her dress. Last night her aunt had
suddenly thrown open the lid of her biggest chest, and
inside was a purple gown she planned to wear for the
feast, and a white damask, embroidered with red flowers
over the high bodice and along the hem, that Cecily might
wear if it fitted. Dear Meg had seen to that, and now she
was struggling to get it fastened while Cecily fidgeted with
impatience to run down to the hall. She saw the visitors
from her window—Lewis in the lead, wearing two
pheasant's feathers in what was most certainly a new red
cap, and with a lute slung on his shoulder. Then came the
priest, Sir James, whom Cecily had not yet spoken to, and
Master Orlebar with his sister riding pillion.

'Hurry! Hurry, Meg!' cried Cecily.

'There—that's the last. Wait, now, till I brush your
hair. Lord, how it shine!' Meg said, admiring as always.
'What I'd give for such a head!'

There was a little embroidered hat to match the dress—
such, indeed, as her own mother might have worn, set
back off the forehead and tied under the chin. It should
have had a floating veil, but when they took it from the
chest the veil fell into wisps and had to be thrown away.
Meg frisked Cecily's long fair hair back behind her ears
and pulled the hat snug, then brushed and brushed till
Cecily thought she would never be done.

'Let him wait, lady,' said Meg in a whisper, close by
Cecily's ear. 'Be still a moment more.'

Cecily stood still, then, her mind brimming with mysteries—not least how she had put her rigorous upbringing away from her with such speed and ease that when Meg at last said 'There!' Cecily turned and embraced her. She kissed her on the cheek, warmly and confidently. 'Dear Meg, dear Meg—a happy, happy Christmas!'

Then she whisked up her skirts and ran from the room, flying as fast as she could to the hall where the company was gathered.

The place seemed packed with people and the talk and the laughter was rising every minute. Bet and Janet, Mary Butterwick and Agnes Bunce were carrying round jugs of steaming wassail. Tom and Anis Bostel stood on the outskirts of the crowd, modestly smiling, but red-bearded Henty counted no man his better, and his was the loudest laugh.

Cecily saw Lewis at once, standing out of the crowd as though painted in colours sharper, bolder, stronger than anyone present. And he saw her, but waited in a mannerly fashion as she moved to her aunt's side.

Dame Elizabeth in her purple gown was a different woman from the one Cecily knew. She had exchanged her plain cap for a tallish head dress with a turned-back front. Round her neck she wore a fine jewel on a thick gold chain, and there were rings on her fingers. She looked handsome as Cecily would never have believed possible and her gracious manner with her guests was full of courtesy and hospitality.

'And here is my good niece, Sir James,' Dame Elizabeth said to the priest standing at her side. She took Cecily's hand and drew her forward. 'I have turned her into a country girl and I dare to claim that she is ten times more content than when she first came. Is it so, Cecily?'

'Yes, dear madam—oh yes, indeed! But twenty times,

not ten!' And just as in the warmth that filled her she had
embraced Meg, so now she pressed her cheek to her
aunt's hand, not only in gratitude, but with an affection
she would never have believed it possible to feel for so
forthright a lady. Then quickly she made her courtesy to
the chaplain.

'Bless you, my dear child,' he said, in a good easy voice
that reminded her of the London days. 'Bless you at this
Yuletide and at all other times. My pupil has spoken of
you.'

'And he has spoken of you, father,' she said. She looked
with interest at his keen dark eyes, at the creases in his
cheeks that proved he laughed often. Here, she saw at
once, was another friend should she need one.

Then there was Roger Orlebar to be greeted, and
Jenufer, whose manner today was inclined unfortunately
towards the wistful. Cecily felt uneasy with her, but Davy,
who was running among the guests with the freedom of a
lap dog, hung on her hand and leant against her skirts
and seemed ready to stay with her all day.

Now she had done her duty and greeted everyone, and
nothing need keep her any longer from giving Lewis his
due. She held out her hand and he took the tips of her
fingers and bowed extravagantly, till his hair fell into his
eyes and he seemed on the point of over-balancing.

'What a fine lady you are today, Cecily Jolland!'

'And how fine a gentleman you have grown, Lewis
Mallory!'

He was wearing a short padded jerkin that was as out
of fashion as her own dress, but he had on new hose of a
matching green, and the points of his shoes were well
stuffed with straw—he would fall over them, he said,
unless he walked all day on his heels.

'If Dame Elizabeth allows,' he said, 'we might have
some music. I have brought my lute, and we have three

recorders—two for my cousins and one for Sir James. Or you may play instead of Cousin Jenufer—she's in a doubtful frame of mind today. But I think you should dance in that gown.'

'Oh I will play—I will play!' she cried. 'But let it be your lute, Master Yaffle, if you please. I have missed mine.' Made even bolder by his smile she added, 'And I will sing.'

'The woodpecker and the lark in concert,' he said. His eyebrows shot up. 'You look so startled—why?'

'For no reason that I know.' The lark—the lark . . . 'They are going to table,' she said.

Sir James spoke a brief and friendly grace that all might understand, not the Latin gabble that Friar Paul would have given them. Then they sat down, all manner of them comfortably settled, and the feast began.

From this moment the day began to race towards its end, its delights so many, its warmth so manifest that there was not time enough to hold it. Dame Elizabeth sat at the head of her table with Sir James on her right and Master Orlebar on her left. Next to the priest sat silent Jenufer, and next to Roger Orlebar came Cecily. Then Nicholas Forge beside Jenufer, with Anis Bostel on his right. And best of all, on Cecily's left sat Lewis Mallory, waved to his seat by Dame Elizabeth in a most friendly fashion. Under the table was Davy, shuttling from side to side, from Cecily to Jenufer, who fed him titbits when he tugged their skirts. On down the table on either side sat Henty and Henty's son and daughter, Tom Bostel, Forge's old mother, who would not stay at home, with Goody Ann, the Bostels' older children, and the maids who served and then sat down, then leapt up again to carry other dishes—till Cecily wondered if they had a chance to eat at all.

It was a day like no other Cecily Jolland had ever

known, a day free and friendly, bound only by kindliness and good manners. When the meal was over at last, the board cleared and taken away, they had their music, changing the instruments about. So first it was Sir James who played the third recorder and Nicholas Forge who took the lute, while Cecily and Lewis, Meg and Henty, Tom and Anis danced. Then Lewis played his lute, the recorders went to Henty, to Tom and to Jenufer, while Roger Orlebar led out Dame Elizabeth. At first she had refused, saying she was too old for dancing; but the sight of the first round added to the pleasures of good food, good wine and good company, changed her mind. The grand lady in the purple gown began to lose her great dignity and to laugh and stamp with the rest. She and Roger Orlebar danced alone, an unexpectedly fine pair of performers, while all the company but the musicians clapped out the rhythm, singing la-la-la because there were no other words.

'Now take the lute, Cecily,' Lewis said; he had called her by her name before, but not in company. 'Sing, as you promised you would.'

'Maybe none of the others wants to hear. . . .'

'Yes, sing—sing!' cried Dame Elizabeth, fallen back in her chair and fanning herself fast. 'I have heard you about the house. I know you have a voice.'

Only the pleasure she had in fingering the lute again and feeling the music plucked from its belly, gave Cecily the courage that she needed. Lewis placed a stool for her in the middle of the hall, and there she sat, with the rest waiting to hear her. Moll Thomsett and those who had been helping in the kitchen came to stand at the door. Silence fell. In the silence the lute answered Cecily's fingers. Whether they knew it there or not, she sang for sheer joy of the occasion. First she sang for Christmas, then she sang for winter—songs that she and Alys had learnt together long ago. Then she sang of returning spring and all things green, of birds singing and the renewing year—

> *Gay comes the singer*
>   *With a song,*
> *Sing we all together,*
>   *All things young;*
> *Field and wood and fallow,*
>   *Lark at dawn,*
> *Young rooks cawing, cawing,*
>   *Philomel*
> *Still complaining of the ancient wrong.*
>
> *Twitters now the swallow,*
>   *Swans are shrill*
>   *Still remembering sorrow,*
> *Cuckoo, cuckoo, goes the cuckoo calling*
>   *On the wooded hill.*
>
> *The birds sing fair,*
>   *Shining earth,*
>   *Gracious after travail,*
>   *Of new birth,*
> *Lies in radiant light,*
>   *Fragrant air.*
>
> *Broad spreads the lime,*
>   *Bough and leaf,*
> *Underfoot the thyme,*
>   *Green the turf.*
>
> *Here come the dances,*
>   *In the grass*
> *Running water glances,*
>   *Murmurs past.*

Happy is the place,
Whispering
Through the open weather
Blow the winds of spring.

One song led to another, until they were singing all together, a carol for the season. All joined hands and danced in a slow circle, singing as they went.

Then suddenly the day was long over, dark at the dooɪ, and the guests far from home. While they feasted the wind had increased. It blew now strongly across the forest, fiercely north, and already it carried some snow.

'Now comes the true winter,' said Roger Orlebar. 'Who knows when we shall be together again?'

'If only the snow were fierce already,' cried Cecily, 'the whole company must stay at Mantlemass!'

'Then we could play and sing away the winter,' Orlebar replied, laughing his deep-chested laugh.

'Well, we shall have music some time in the spring,' Sir James said, looking from one to the other as Lewis and Cecily stood together, spinning out words of goodbye. 'You, my dear daughter Cecily, shall come with my pupil to the palace chapel. There I have my viol, and a rebeck. Between us we might do very well.'

'Master Yaffle shall show me the way, Father.'

'Jesu have you in his keeping, child,' said the priest. 'And may he bring us an early spring.'

'Amen,' said Lewis and Cecily both together; and very devoutly.

Though it was time to part the company lingered, for all by now were flushed and gay. The maids scurried about the hall, Forge and Bostel and Henty pursuing them for Christmas forfeits. So, too, the rest embraced as they parted, laughing. Dame Elizabeth offered her cheek to Master Orlebar, and Jenufer was kissed smackingly by

Henty, once he had dealt with Meg and Mary, Agnes and Janet and Bet.

'I brought you a Christmas token,' Lewis said to Cecily, 'and I have forgotten to give it to you. It is here safe in my pouch.' He brought out a small flat object wrapped in a piece of cloth, and handed it to her with a bow.

She unwrapped the little pack and found inside five small bright feathers, two greeny-yellow, two speckled brown and white, one red—and all clipped together with a pin to make an ornament.

'The smith made the pin. It is true steel. You know the feathers?'

'The woodpecker. The yaffle . . . Thank you,' said Cecily, so quietly she hardly heard herself speak, 'thank you for your care and kindness.'

Lewis took her by the hand. Bending forward and smiling, he kissed her quickly on the brow.

8
Snowfall to Spring

In the winter days, with the snow piled high against the walls, the windows fretted with icy patterns, Dame Elizabeth set herself to teach Cecily to read. She was too high-tempered and sharp-tongued to make a good teacher; while Cecily, an unaccustomed pupil, was frightened out of her wits by the immensity of the task. Dame Elizabeth banged with her fists in sheer frustration, Cecily wept at her own stupidity. Quite awe-struck, Meg and Mary Butterwick sat in the background stitching at coney skins. Meg was all sympathy for Cecily; but Mary felt that Dame Elizabeth was poorly rewarded for taking such pains.

Each morning Cecily opened her bed curtains and

called to Davy as she had once called to Alys. The little
boy ran on bare feet over the cold floor to the window. He
blew on the obscuring frost until there was a hole big
enough to peer through. Each morning Cecily hoped to
hear a cry of excitement that would tell her the snow was
melting; but the winter went on and on with no sign of
respite. There were bright and brittle days when the
house and the surrounding forest looked like some
splendid table decoration—one of those delicate inven-
tions of spun sugar that the master cooks called *subtleties*,
that sparkled and glittered in intricate designs. But the
sun made no impression on the depth and hardness of the
snow. What dropped from the trees was replaced over-
night, and the drifts grew constantly higher and more
treacherous.

Mantlemass was a place under siege—a world cut off
from every other world and subsisting on itself. It was so
for every household about the forest—Ghylls Hatch, the
weaver's place, the forges with their stone dwelling-
houses close at hand, the small huddled cottages of the
charcoal burners and the iron workers—all kept their own
counsel and existed on what stores had been gathered in.
Mantlemass was well provided and those who lived and
worked there might count themselves fortunate. For the
rest, with little with which to supply themselves and less
space for keeping, the outlook as the winter lengthened
became bleak. The deer languished and the birds died on
the branches, hares and rabbits fell to the foxes prowling
and crying in the bitter nights. There could hardly have
been less food for the taking. Cecily thought of the coney
warrens, where the Mantlemass animals were nourished
for the profit of their pelts; it must be bitter for half
starving foresters to know of all that pampered meat. But
for the depth of the drifts, the warrens would surely have
been raided.

Sometimes Cecily walked out fifty yards or so with Davy, on the few hard paths that had been dug again and again and trampled by the men about the place. The snow on all sides was scored and pitted by innumerable prints—not of men, who could not venture there, but of birds and small animals. Mice made tracks so delicate they were like the frost patterns on the inside of the windows. Birds of all sorts and sizes scrabbled for dropped berries, or rested their exhausted breasts against the snow, leaving an imprint light and despairing. The owls flurried a yard or more of the surface when they swooped after mice and birds; once Cecily found the strangest mark of all, made by the stiff short tail feathers of the woodpecker, as he rocked back off his claws that had not been made for the ground but for the bark of trees.

The feathered pin that Lewis had given Cecily at Christmas she wore always as a talisman, and it was like some magic key to these small signs scratched on the surface of the winter. It was she who showed Davy where the fox had loped his almost single track, where rabbits had sprung from their strong hindquarters to their modest forepaws. This was a language in itself, a reading that needed no learning and that gave her greater pleasure than what she must learn from books and Dame Elizabeth. It made the winter bearable, and because she could teach Davy what she knew, she recovered from the humiliation of finding it difficult to be taught herself.

At Ghylls Hatch the winter was a more uncomfortable experience than at Mantlemass. The house was older, draughtier, the winter provisions were not even half so well ordered. Jenufer huddled by the fire and cried because her bones ached with the cold, the servants complained of short commons, and Lewis groaned with boredom. He could neither get to his lessons with the priest, nor find excuses to visit Mantlemass, nor do half the work he needed to with the horses. With enormous effort the yard was cleared of snow each morning, and that was the only place where the animals could be exercised. One heavy fall and then nights of frost would have been easier to deal with than each night's snow soft-piled on yesterday's. To make matters worse, a young stallion had broken out of his stall and careered into a snow drift, breaking both forelegs; a great loss, for Lewis had planned to use him for the lame mare, Iris, who would be ready to breed in the spring. This, added to the loss of Zephyr, caused great gloom at Ghylls Hatch.

It was the deepest winter Lewis could remember, and the only comfort he got from it was the knowledge that the most determined father could not carry his daughter away at such a time. As for how the world was going, and whether indeed Sir Thomas Jolland might safely venture back to his own country, there was no means of knowing. In the first days of the snow, before it deepened and drifted, Friar Paul had asked for shelter at Ghylls Hatch and slept the night there. He had been about the countryside as far as the outskirts of London, and his story was that the land was quiet—though he had been told of trials and executions actually in the city. None could confirm if this was fact or legend and it was little enough to go on. None the less, the friar had been convinced that civil strife had reached its end and its only legacy among the people was a fear of disbanded soldiery. Even at this date, nearly five months after that final battle on Bosworth Field, there were still soldiers without employment wandering at large. After the proclamation of the new king many of his soldiers had been absorbed into the work of the harvest and so slipped back into everyday life. But some remained, of the kind that were vagrant by nature; and these might be feared, for they would plunder or kill as the occasion suggested.

'But winter will cool them,' Friar Paul had said, 'and by spring they will be dispersed or dead—who knows which?'

Such wandering bands sought places like the forest for shelter and hiding; but the foresters were far too jealous of their own rights in the place to stomach poachers—though they would harbour a fugitive whatever his crime.

For Lewis the short days were too long, the long nights full of uneasy dreams. Now separated from Cecily he had time to understand what had befallen him, and he was torn with doubt and distrust, with jealousy of those who saw her daily, with anxiety that she might not think of him as he thought of her; with a bitter fear that even if she did think so, they would be kept apart. And yet how freely Dame Elizabeth had seemed to encourage their friendship. This, in itself, made Lewis uneasy. Why had she done so? Was it because she found him so far below her niece that there could be no thought or fear of any union? But she knew him to be of good stock—better, in the world's eyes, than her own. Then was it because she schemed to see Cecily out of harm's way—out of her father's way, that was—by settling her before Sir Thomas came or sent to claim her? Well that would please all but her father—so long as it would please Cecily; for Lewis would not have her at all unless she willed it as much as he . . . But at the back of his mind there moved a more subtle fear. He could not quite forget Jenufer's garbled hints about some enmity between the families. He knew from Sir James that Dame Elizabeth had reason to hate her brother, and even an innocent in the ways of the world would recognise her as a woman to whom revenge could be very sweet. Could she, in fact, use Cecily to further that purpose, by encouraging her in pursuits bound to enrage him? He himself had cause to respect Dame Elizabeth, but now he was ready to be suspicious of heaven itself.

There was so much in all this that was mysterious and unexplained, that his doubts grew upon Lewis as he fretted out the winter. In the cold and lonely days, and in the snow-lit nights, his nightmare was that he must lose his happiness almost before it had begun. He could bear his own heartbreak, as any man must—but how, if indeed she loved him, would he also bear Cecily's?

With all this turning and churning in his heart and mind, Lewis woke one night after an hour in his bed, and knew that the wind had changed. It was blowing from the south-west and the thaw had begun.

Cecily, too, when she woke in the darkness heard the almost forgotten sound of water dripping from the roof.

'In two days,' said Dame Elizabeth next morning, 'it will be spring.'

It was true. The thaw was fast and complete. The snow was like an army in retreat, fleeing before a strong enemy. The sun shone brilliantly, everything changed. It was a brown sad earth that first appeared, shrivelled by the months of cold and darkness. But within a week the pussy willow catkins showed silver along the gushing rivers, and in a little less than a week more Davy came running with a primrose squashed in his fist.

A week and almost a week were a long time; long because although they brought callers they did not bring the one Cecily looked for. Fourteen days and no sign of Lewis. Perhaps in the long winter he had fallen sick and died, and she would never see him again. She was crushed by her feeling of desolation when he did not appear. It had all been a game and now he was busy

with some other . . . How would she live if either thing
were true?

'Now that the winter is over,' her aunt said one
evening, 'we must consider how the world goes. It is
six months since your father left England.' She grimaced
as she named him. 'We cannot hope that he will fail to
get some word soon to Mantlemass.'

Cecily had begun to tremble and she clasped her hands
together to hide their shaking. 'What word will it be,
madam?'

'What indeed? Either he will have settled himself as
only he knows how; or he will be deeper in trouble than
before. And as I am not able to wish him well,' Dame
Elizabeth said with a rough laugh, 'I wish him with
trouble enough to keep him far away.'

This bold way of talking never failed to make Cecily
pray to heaven not to take her aunt too seriously. If death
or betrayal came to her father, her conscience would have
a hard time with the fact that she had listened to her
aunt's ill-wishing.

'At this time of year,' Dame Elizabeth said, 'I send
Nicholas Forge about my business to London. He is
likely to be two or three weeks away from home. He will
bring us news of how the new king is ruling, and what
changes there are, or likely to be. And if he has no other
means, then he shall go to your uncle Digby to enquire
for news of Sir Thomas.'

'I think my uncle has cast us off altogether,' Cecily
said.

'Well, he may be appealed to if all else fails . . . And so
tomorrow, Cecily, you will oblige me by riding an errand.
I always send to Master Orlebar to know if he has any
commissions for Nicholas. They go to London from
Ghylls Hatch later in the year, with the horses. At this
time the preparation there is so great there's neither man

nor beast about the place that can call his soul or his time
his own.' She looked at Cecily and smiled slightly. 'I am
sorry to send you, child. But there is a great deal to do at
Mantlemass, also, and I cannot spare any of the men.'

Cecily murmured, 'Yes, madam,' her heart leaping into
her throat with pleasure and with dread.

She set off next morning after prayers. Her aunt was
busy with Nicholas Forge, discussing who he must see
when he went to London. Cecily had thought she would
take Davy with her to Ghylls Hatch, but she could not
find him. Since the snow ended he had taken to disappear-
ing for hours on end and nothing would wring from him
where he had been.

The morning was so beautiful that all Cecily's fears
seemed foolish. In the sunshine that had come after a
night of rain, she knew there would be some easy reason
for Lewis's neglect. As she rode away from Mantlemass
she was singing to herself and Cressyd the same song of
spring she had sung so hopefully at Christmas time.
She went up through the woods where she had first seen
Lewis riding, and then took the short way to the main
track leading to Ghylls Hatch. The little path would take
her near the pool where she had talked to him on the day
she went to the weaver's cottage, the first time she ever
rode alone. For sheer pleasure of the memory, she turned
out of her course to pass that way. . . .

He was there. She saw his red cap. And then as she
tried not to smile with pleasure at the sight, she saw him
look up. Himself unsmiling and almost unnaturally pale,
he pulled off his cap and stepped forward. As she shifted
Cressyd down towards the pool, he put out his hand and
laid it on the bridle.

'Where have you been?' he demanded.

'Where . . . ?' Cecily almost gaped in her bewilderment
and outrage. 'Where have *you* been, Lewis Mallory?'

'I have waited for you,' he said sternly, 'day after day.'

'Here?'

'Where else?'

'But this is not precisely where I live. And my aunt's house is not hard to find.'

'I needed to see you here,' he insisted, 'not among your people. I was sure you would come. It has not been easy, I can tell you, escaping day by day. We are all off our feet with work.'

'Well,' she said, defeated, laughing at him for being so absurd, for relieving all her doubts and fears, for being here at all, alive and well and needing to see her. 'Well, I am here. I have come. I have done as you expected me to. And better late than not at all—so my aunt says.'

He lifted her from the saddle. 'I have much to say to you, Cecily Jolland. The winter has been like eternity. I might well have gone out of my mind.'

'I have learnt to read,' she boasted.

'Then your mind has been well occupied.'

'I ought to say—my aunt has been trying to teach me!' She was ready to tease him out of his sombre expression, but she felt unable to mock him at all. 'Look—I am wearing your Christmas token. The feathers are as fine as ever.'

'I said—I have much to say to you. You must stop chattering and listen. And you must answer truly what I ask you. I have been thinking what I must say to you almost since Christmas day. But swear you will answer honestly and steadfastly, not sparing my feelings.'

'Well—I will swear if you wish me to. But I am to be trusted.'

'It came to me suddenly,' he said. 'I knew without warning—or so I thought . . . But then I wondered . . . I could not be certain—not without seeeing you and speaking to you . . . I came here—well, I could not have spoken quietly to you anywhere else . . . You must understand that.'

'Oh Lewis—please! Who's chattering now?'

'If indeed we love one another,' he said flatly, 'then certainly we should be made man and wife.' He frowned deeply. 'This is what I have thought. And you? Now it is in answering that you must be steadfast.'

She delayed a moment, but only for the delight of hearing his words repeating in her head. . . .

'Cecily . . . ?'

'I have thought, too. And now I know I have thought the same as you.'

'And that is the truth? Be very sure of it.'

'I said I would swear. Yes. That is the truth.'

'To be together always.' He was gazing at her, but still not smiling. 'You know they will try to prevent it,' he said harshly. 'You do understand that? They will do all they can to keep us apart. I have thought how your aunt has seemed to draw us together. But it makes no sense to me. It can only be baseless cruelty—would she be cruel? I think she would. Would she let us take hands and then tear us apart?'

'Hush,' she said, amazed by his quiet fury. 'Take hands, then, and swear not to be torn apart. Take hands and swear to hold fast. Forget the rest—and say what you said before.'

'To be together always . . . ?'

'Besides that, you said—'

'That we love each other . . . ?'

'Yes! That. That is the true part. Let it be enough. We need not fear yet—need we? This is a wonderful thing!' she cried, excitement catching her. 'To love at all is most extraordinary. But to love rightly—surely that's a miracle? Only think—that we should have met at all— out of all the world of men and women that we should

be here in this place, both at one time! And that we should
feel the same—each for the other. Oh Lewis—how has it
happened?'

'You are right. It is truly a miracle.'

'We must make a vow that nothing can separate us.
As you vowed to stand between me and trouble—on your
father's ring. Do you remember?'

'I remember the smallest thing that has happened
since I first saw you. I remember nothing else. The rest
has all gone from me—my father's treatment of me, and
the loss of my mother and my brothers—such things
mean nothing to me now. I forgot my childhood when
I came to Ghylls Hatch, and now I have forgotten all the
rest.' He fumbled for the thong round his neck and pulled
out the ring. 'Take it in your hand.'

She did as he told her and as before he closed her
fingers on the ring and then enclosed her hand in his own.

'We must call this our betrothal,' he said. 'I vow to
Cecily Jolland—my dear love—that I will die rather than
be parted from her . . . But I should not have said that.'

'Because I must vow the same?' She shrugged. 'What
else should I vow? I would die anyway, now—without
you. Lord, how the winter dragged!'

He smiled for the first time, and she made the same vow
as he had made. They kissed, solemnly. She was still
holding the ring. She opened her hand and it lay on her
palm. At last she saw the emblem she seemed to have been
seeking, dreaming and waking, through all the days of her
life.

'My pretty bird,' she heard herself say, in her mother's
sighing, just-remembered tones. . . .

There was still Cecily's errand to Master Orlebar, and
they rode to Ghylls Hatch together, the horses stepping
close enough for their riders to take hands. Just within
sight of Ghylls Hatch they moved apart. They had

decided that no one should know of their betrothal, for
the secret seemed too good to share.

No spring had ever seemed so fine. If there were days
when the sun did not shine, then neither was aware of
them. There were days, many of them, when they did
not meet, but it seemed enough that they breathed the
same air. Cecily went daily to the meeting place by the
pool, and mostly Lewis contrived to get there, too, though
their visits did not always coincide. Whoever was there
first left a token—a mark scratched in the bark of the
sturdiest tree. Whichever of them found a fresh mark
then cancelled it with a second.

There was a lot of work for Lewis at this time of the
year. The clearing-up and mucking-out after the winter
was a colossal task, and there were the mares in foal
needing extra care. In May twenty or so horses would
be taken to London for sale—perhaps to the royal stable,
where they were needed whatever the name of the king,
or else to be disposed of in the open market. Lewis had
never accompanied his cousin on these annual expeditions,
but this year he was determined he would go. With Cecily
to strengthen him he felt twice himself. Because his mind
was full of plans—even plans to carry her off, if need be,
and go to some far place where no one could find them—
his manner began to change, becoming within a few days
twice as assertive. To the youthful spring of his long-
legged stride was added the aggressiveness of a boy
moving suddenly and positively into manhood. Now his
life had found its purpose and his self-doubts fell from
him like an old coat.

It was not long before he realised that his cousin was
watching him curiously. He said nothing until Lewis
asked if he might go to London with the horses.

'Far better not,' said Roger Orlebar. 'There's little

there to interest you.' The loud laugh that interrupted him made him frown. 'There's neither sense nor manners in that, boy. It's not my task to take you to the world, but rather to keep you out of it.'

'That's blunt, at least.' Lewis's laughter died and he began to feel something of the helpless anger that had plagued him as a child in his early years at Ghylls Hatch. 'I have put up with my father's roughness—*why* he disowned me seemed no matter. But I'll ask you now— now that I'm grown and got some sense—why? Why?'

'You may ask. It'll do little good if you do. I was never told.'

'You took me in—and never knew why you had to do so?'

'Your father was my kinsman.' Orlebar's dark weathered skin began to redden. 'Well—if it must be said . . . I was poor and struggling to make a living here. I was proud of his trust perhaps—a man of his standing in the world . . . Also he rewarded me handsomely . . . And before you accuse me, Lewis—I was unwilling and I was bribed— but it is not by your father's wealth that I have been re-paid. I think you know you have become as dear as a son to me.'

Lewis looked briefly into his cousin's troubled face, and as briefly smiled. He fumbled after the right words. 'And I . . . And you. . . .'

'Then,' said Roger Orlebar, smiling in his turn, 'I shall speak to you as a father must. You are too much concerned with Dame Elizabeth's young niece.'

'Dame Elizabeth has not said so.'

'Dame Elizabeth FitzEdmund is a law unto herself. We both know that. What her purposes are no man rightly knows. But there are things I do know—that you and the girl meet about the forest—that you have been seen riding together—'

'Where's the harm in that?'

'Lewis, you must attend to me. One thing I know, for all my ignorance—between your father and Sir Thomas Jolland there is something deep and dangerous.'

'What thing? And how do you know?'

'From words dropped. From one certain happening. I know this—that at one time these men were brothers in arms, that they fought under the same standard—both were for Lancaster, both were close to the king. But then, when things were going badly, Sir Thomas turned his coat and fawned on the Duke of York. When York became king of England, Sir Thomas was very well placed.'

'Less well when that king died at Bosworth!'

'The girl's the daughter of a traitor. It is preposterous for your father's son to think of her. Mallorys have been pillars of the Lancastrian cause. You know that at least about your own people?'

'They are not my people any more . . . From words dropped, you said, and from *one certain happening*. What was that?'

'Before he brought you here, your father took you to connections of your mother's—and afterwards he moved you here.'

'I remember that much,' said Lewis, bitterly recalling his misery.

'That was in Buckinghamshire—and there was a manor two miles or so from where you were left. It was one of several granted by the crown to Dame Elizabeth's husband—you know he was the son of a royal duke, though born on the wrong side of the blanket, as they say. When your father discovered Dame Elizabeth was living there—and she was there briefly—then he fetched you away. There's the measure of what Mallory owes Jolland in the way of love.'

'And brought me here?' Lewis said incredulously. 'Where also Dame Elizabeth has a manor?'

'Mantlemass had stood empty since it was built. There wasn't one of us about here knew who the owner was. When your father questioned me about my neighbours— and how he did question me!—I answered with entire honesty. I told him freely everything I knew. It was six months and more after that before Mantlemass was lived in, and its dame proved to be Elizabeth Fitz-Edmund.

'And if you had told my father then—you would have lost what he had given you.'

'Not a material loss only. Believe that.'

'I do believe it. But if you are my father now—then I am Orlebar, not Mallory. And what reason has Orlebar to frown on an alliance with Jolland?'

'No, Lewis, no!' his cousin cried. 'This is bold beyond words! Alliance, indeed! I gave a solemn undertaking to your father . . . ' He threw up his hands and turned away impatiently. 'Let that suffice, boy! Let that suffice.'

Bitterly troubled, Lewis watched him stride off towards the stables. He had always shown himself good, kind and honest. Today he had stopped short of final candour. Lewis had no doubt in mind that there was something more his cousin could have told him.

Just as Lewis was much occupied with his work in the spring weather, so Cecily had her hands full of jobs about the house. The linen must be looked to and repaired and the bed curtains taken down to be beaten and hung in the sun. Outside, the warrens were undisturbed at this time for the creatures were lustily breeding. The cattle were turned out by day and the muck racked from the byres until the midden grew as high as the neighbouring barns. There were already two new calves and the lambing pens were full. Davy ran from place to place as the days increased the young stock; but he still vanished for hours together and Cecily had given up trying to discover where he went.

Now between Cecily and her aunt there existed a curious quiet. No confidences were given, nor were they sought. Cecily knew that her aunt watched her, but with a distant contemplation that seemed to suggest a standing back from events. She did not speak again of her brother's possible return, but when Nicholas Forge had not returned from London at the end of three weeks, she grew restless.

'He should be back. He must have taken some sickness and been delayed.'

'You said he had much to do for you.'

'Yes, so he has. I am impatient. He has taken a petition for me, too. Now that we have a new king I need to confirm my rights in Mantlemass. Then I may be certain it will go to my appointed heir.'

'Then he is sitting day by day in some ante-room,' decided Cecily. 'For I do remember my father saying it took time to get the king's ear.'

As she spoke she wondered briefly if she might be her aunt's heir, as she now knew she was her mother's. And because she was in a state to dream, she dreamt of living there at Mantlemass with Lewis and seeing their children grow in the place. She longed to confide in her aunt, then. She would look for Lewis tomorrow, she decided; she would look all day until she found him, and tell him they must no longer keep her aunt in ignorance of how things stood between them.

The next day was warm and misty, the sun held behind a haze of thin cloud. The forest steamed. The ground was now thick with flower, anemones and promroses lingering as the first bluebells shot above them. Cecily went on foot to the meeting place. He was not there and he had left no sign since yesterday, when he had carved a crescent in the tree trunk and she had later carved it into two against his next visit.

If he had not been yet, then he would almost certainly come later, and she sat down to wait. In the complete stillness of the misty day she heard every sound with a startling and beautiful clarity. Birds fidgeted and sang. A stoat ran by and paused, rearing up rigid as a stick till her quiet soothed him and he went on his way. And for the first time since she had come to the forest, she saw a snake slide by. She watched it carefully, ready to leap up and fly from the place; but it was a green grass snake, mild as milk, moving harmlessly across the path.

It was long past noon when she heard the sound she was waiting for. Lewis came riding down the track on Diamante, and the moment she looked at him she knew that something was wrong.

'Nothing is changed,' Cecily said positively, when Lewis had told his tale. She was frightened by his gloom. 'Why did you tell your cousin what we had sworn to keep secret? I longed to tell my aunt, but I did not.'

'There was no need to tell him. He knew. It was in my face, no doubt. I daresay I have never looked like this before.'

'But nothing—nothing—is changed,' she insisted. 'Your father has left you all these years—why should he care that I am my father's daughter? What can it matter to us if they are enemies?'

'We are bound to suffer for their pride and ambitions; for their revenge. In law we are still children, and they will part us for their own purposes. Yes—even your aunt.'

'Oh no, Lewis—no. She promised me happiness. Now that I know her, I believe in her deeply. If we confide in her, who knows, she may help us.'

9

'It is too dangerous. Your father still has more power over you than she has.'

'Why should he not abandon me—as yours has abandoned you?'

Lewis shook his head. 'I am thinking what could happen to you if he learnt what we intend—'

'What could happen?' she asked, holding his hands tightly. But she knew, she had known since that afternoon in the orchard, in that other life. 'My aunt in York . . . The abbess. . . .'

'He would do it—wouldn't he?'

'If it suited him . . .You mean we had best be married and forestall him? We must do that. They cannot part us then. They dare not.'

'You have twice my courage. I'm ashamed. My cousin has still not told me all he knows—I am sure of that. But let it go. That's another world—the world of great men. We can turn our backs on them and keep our roots and our roof here in the forest.'

'Then go to Sir James, Lewis. Ask him to help us. He is the one who can save us.'

'I'll go to him this evening. You go home now, Cecily. And if you must tell your aunt—then do so. You will know what is best, though I would sooner keep the secret.'

Cecily did not go directly to Mantlemass. She watched Lewis ride away and then sat a long time by the water. She held her head between her clenched fists, trying desperately to think what was best, wondering whether to ask her aunt for help, wondering what Sir James would say to Lewis—for after all he had a duty, too, to her guardian and to Lewis's. She sat with closed eyes, praying desperately that she need not lose her happiness. When at last she could neither think nor pray any more, she got up stiffly and started for home. Halfway there,

Davy ran out of the bushes and threw himself against her skirt. She took his hand and they went home together.

The mist had thickened as the day declined, and it was many hours now since Cecily had gone in search of Lewis. As she reached the house she saw Sim Carter leading away a bay horse. That meant that Nicholas Forge had returned. Bringing with him—what news? There was a second horse that she did not recognise, tethered near the door. She went into the hall, with Davy still hanging on to her hand. Her aunt was there, and two men with her. One was Nicholas Forge.

The other, who turned as she entered, was her father's servant, Giles, who had ridden with him into exile last September.

9
The Marriage

Cecily saw at once that Giles had bettered himself. He no longer wore the livery of a serving-man but a sober respectable suit that suggested a gentleman's steward or secretary. She remembered that he had spoken to her kindly on the ride from London to Mantlemass, and that she had answered shrewishly. His face had changed since then, as well as his clothes. He was lean, upright, bold, and his eyes were those of a self-seeker. No doubt he had learnt from his master.

Of all this Dame Elizabeth, too, would be well aware. Her shrewd, ironic dignity dominated the hall.

'Your father has sent this man with a message, niece. We had best hear what it is.'

'His secretary, madam,' said Giles, looking round for his master's daughter. He had glanced at Cecily without any recognition as she came indoors, a girl in a plain gown with a small boy hanging on to her hand. He looked so shocked at the change in her that she almost laughed in his face.

'Good day to you, Giles,' she said. From this moment she was calm. She had everything to gain or to lose and she needed all her wits about her.

'Lady,' said Giles in a mourning tone, dropping on his knee and taking her hand as if to kiss it. 'You have been sorely treated! Alas, that your father's daughter should be so humbled!'

'Alas, that my father's servant should be so bold!' she retorted, snatching away her hand. For a second it looked as if she might lay it about his cheek and he ducked his head involuntarily, so that she laughed. 'What's your message?' she demanded.

'Madam—I am to say to you that Sir Thomas is well-settled in France, and shall remain there. That he has two good tidings for you and awaits your return under his roof.'

'I am my aunt's ward and must abide by her wishes.'

'You are your father's daughter, lady,' he repeated virtuously. 'I have told you his wishes.'

'Doubtless you have some written instruction from your master?' Dame Elizabeth said.

'Why—no, madam. But I have my own years of service to Sir Thomas—the lady Cecily knows me well and can vouch for me.'

'You speak very prettily, I must say, considering your earlier place with my brother—were you not one of his grooms? No doubt Sir Thomas would gladly be reunited with his daughter. But are you to be her escort?'

'Sir Thomas expects that her maid will attend her, naturally—'

'Oh, we are quite differently placed here, Master

Giles. My girls are far too simple to travel from home, and in any event I cannot spare a single one of them.'

'Pray tell your master,' said Cecily, 'that I am very content where he placed me.' She gave her aunt a rather sly look as she spoke, and Dame Elizabeth returned her glance, straight-faced and straight-backed. After all the dread of how such a summons as this might come, the uneasy presence of one man seemed almost frivolous.

Giles was looking at Cecily with his eyebrows drawn together and his mouth down at the corners. He had never heard her speak so much before, and her voice must seem to belong to another. What a tale to take back to his master! The delicate girl turned to a sturdy wench ready to stamp on his toes if he did not keep them out of the way . . . 'You spoke of two good tidings—were those your words?' she said. 'What tidings?'

'Sir Thomas is to give you a new mother, lady.'

This time he made the sensation he wished. He heard with obvious satisfaction Dame Elizabeth's abrupt, derisive exclamation.

'And has she great estates?' she demanded. 'And titles? Sir Thomas has lacked titles. His last attempt to gain some went astray.'

'The lady is a widow of a French nobleman, and has indeed her own titles. Of her three brothers, one has the ear of the French King, the second is a cardinal, and the third is as fair as the day . . . .'

'Indeed!' Dame Elizabeth's voice was icy sharp. 'Then this time Sir Thomas is well-settled. What do you think of this, Cecily?'

'I wish him every joy,' said Cecily, her eyes on her folded hands. 'Though I thought he was true to my mother's memory. He always told me so.'

'A good way of saving himself for better times, no doubt,' said her aunt. 'Memory is a sad companion. Be

generous, Cecily. Relieve the lady of a stepdaughter—
women seldom love such a relation.'

'Sir Thomas has made his plans, madam,' Giles said.
'I have not told you the rest. Two good tidings, I said.
So here is the second.' He looked at Cecily and smiled.
'You may rejoice, lady. Your father has chosen you a fine
husband.'

Cecily did not remember leaving the hall and going to
her own room. But she was there now, lying in her bed,
with Meg and Mary crowding round, and Davy sitting
near her feet with his black eyes starting out of his head.

'Ah, no wonder she took swimey, poor soul,' Mary was
saying, 'the way he talk . . . Why don't she wake? Oh she
look very particular, Meg!'

Particular meant unwell, and Cecily, trying vainly to
force her eyes open, murmured protestingly 'I am neither
swimey nor particular, so hold your tongues, the pair of you.'

'Run down quick, Mary, and tell the mistress our
young lady's come to her senses.'

Cecily did not protest this time. She was in her night-
gown, so the girls must have undressed her and put her
to bed, and that would have taken time. Perhaps she had
fainted, but she could not remember it. She had wanted so
desperately to escape from Giles and his hateful smiling
words that her senses seemed simply to have released her
and wafted her from the room. But the words had indeed
been spoken, and there was no true escape from them.

'Meg . . .'

'Yes, my dear sweet lady?' answered Meg, taking
Cecily's hand and stroking it.

'Has he gone?'

'Yes, he has. He made a fine belver, but she sent him
off. Oh her voice—you should've heard! Chizzly as old
grit, it sounded.'

Now Cecily could close her eyes no longer. She sat up in bed. 'He'll come again, Meg. What shall we do?' Sick of discretion, she cried out, 'You know the only one I'll ever marry!'

'I see that—oh, long ago I see that, as I think you know. And night and morning, ever since, I pray for your happiness.'

'I will be happy!' cried Cecily, clenching her teeth and gripping Meg's hand so hard that she had to pull it away. 'I will be! I will be!'

'Hush—that's a mawkin face. Look—you frit poor Davy.'

'The uglier I look, the better. That fellow thought me sadly changed, thank God. Noblemen do not marry with country girls and they cannot re-make me twice. What if I stained my face and hands and sheared off my hair? That should frit *him*, Meg.'

'That's wild talk, I'd say.'

'But did you hear? My father is to marry—and I am to have the lady's brother for my husband! It cannot even be decent . . . Perhaps it will not be allowed. . . .'

'He'll save you,' Meg said softly. 'Your lovely lad— him, Lewis Mallory. And all here shall help him. True enough, you do have a bit of a foresty look these last months. Now here's where your home is. You'll see how the forest won't care to give you up.'

'My father's a powerful man . . . Oh God help me!'

'Here's your good aunt come to you,' Meg said, moving respectfully away from the bedside.

'Leave the room now, Meg,' Dame Elizabeth said. 'And take that boy with you. And when the door closes, keep your ear from the keyhole.'

'I never do anything but that!'

'And your eye, too, Meg, if you please.'

Meg called to Davy and flounced away. Cecily lay

back and watched her aunt walking the room, her head bent, her hands clasped tightly together. Cecily had grown very accustomed to what had shocked her—Dame Elizabeth's dominating manner, her loud firm voice and its mockery, her ease with the men about the place, her quick coarse humour. It was a surprise to see her, as she seemed now, at a loss for words.

'Tell me what I must do,' Cecily said, to break the silence.

Dame Elizabeth came to the bed and sat down. 'Nicolas Forge has told me that Sir Thomas is thought to be in England. Your uncle Digby parted with this news after much soliciting. He could not say where, but it probably would be safer for him not to know. There's no welcome for Sir Thomas in his own country for the present, that's sure.'

'Where might he be?' asked Cecily faintly, half glancing over her shoulder as though she expected him to be already at the door.

'No nearer than the coast, I daresay. He'll be in harbour, waiting to take the first tide after Giles brings you to him.'

'But I am not to go with him, madam? You would never send me . . . ?'

'No, no—my dear child, you must learn to trust me. But he'll come again, Cecily. And a second time he will not come alone.'

'Then—who will come with him?'

'Your father could venture as far as this, no doubt. Once he reaches the forest he's almost certainly secure. But you are not to fear him. I have promised you—have I not promised you time and time again that you are to be happy?'

'But have you mocked me, madam?' Cecily's voice rose dangerously as despair touched her. 'I have thought and thought of all your riddles and your mysteries that you would not explain. I know you hate my father and I know why. But I can see you might be revenged on him through me. I have tried not to see it. But it is too plain.'

'Why, yes, I might do so. But can you think I would? Is this all you have learnt of me?'

Cecily burst into loud and bitter tears. 'Why—why have you let me make Lewis Mallory my dearest friend? I know now that his father and mine are enemies. And you know it. Is this indeed your purpose—to plague Sir Thomas through me and my misery?'

Dame Elizabeth caught Cecily by the wrists and shook her.

'What would he care for your misery? It is through your happiness I shall pay my account . . . Cecily—answer me truly. Is he—young Mallory—is he indeed your dearest friend, as you call him?'

'As I am his! And always will be! And if we are parted we cannot live! This is the only truth I know and if you take it from me—I must die.'

'Hush, now! You will make yourself ill. I need you calm and sensible.'

'How can I be? I understand nothing. I don't know who I may trust. I am afraid of everyone, except Lewis. Of everyone—everyone!'

'Oh be quiet and listen to me!' Now Dame Elizabeth had Cecily by the shoulders, alternately soothing and shouting, but with no effect. 'Be calm! Even now I could fail in what I have planned all these years—yes, years, Cecily. We must know what we are doing. Are you listening to me?'

Cecily was now past reason. She could not have stopped sobbing if she had wished to, and she was so far gone in misery that she did not care. Her aunt released her, and she fell back, her eyes closed, but the tears pouring under her lashes and soaking the pillow.

Dame Elizabeth was at the door, calling, 'Meg! Where are you? Come here to me, girl.'

Meg's voice came faintly up the stairs. 'You did say I should take my eyes and ears away. . . .'

'That'll do. Bring me a cup of the wine posset. The herb receipt—you will know the one. And get about it sharply—there's no time to waste.' She returned to the bedside and tried again to quiet Cecily. 'You will make yourself ill, I tell you!'

Meg came scuttling with a covered cup, and Dame Elizabeth took it and sniffed at it.

'This is strong, Meg. But maybe that is best. I must speak to her and then she can sleep, and tomorrow we must act as best we can.' She was talking to herself more than to Meg, whose sympathetic face was pink and tearful at the sight of Cecily. 'Hold it for her, Meg. Come now, niece. Drink it down.'

The first mouthful made Cecily gasp, it was so strong. She remembered the drink. Her aunt had given it to her the night she arrived at Mantlemass, then as now beside herself with misery. It had made her sleep and dream the old dream. She drank obediently enough, her tears checked. The soothing herbs acted quickly and she sighed and lay back drained and exhausted.

'Now listen carefully,' Dame Elizabeth said, bending over Cecily after Meg had gone away reluctantly. 'I will tell you now why your father kept you so close, and then we will thank God together that you were left here because it was convenient to a threatened man. You are sleepy already. Then take this comfort with you for the night: before you can be married to this nobleman of France— this husband of your father's cunning choice—vows must be cancelled and contracts set aside. Do you hear what I am saying?'

Cecily murmured something. The draft was so strong

it was like a blow between the eyes. The bitter taste of it was still in her mouth but she was already drowsy. She had difficulty in keeping her eyes open and her aunt's face swam and blurred before her.

'Your father has been very patient. He has waited years for what even he can hardly have hoped for—a cardinal! A cardinal for a brother-in-law! Are you listening?'

'A cardinal . . .'

'He needs such a man—he needs a sympathetic churchman who will speak for him in the only possible quarter. You cannot marry without a papal dispensation. Do you understand? *Do you understand?* That fool, Meg—however much of the foxglove did she use? It could be poison! Cecily!' Again she had her by the shoulders, shaking her, gently at first then much harder. 'You must listen to me. The Pope will be petitioned to release you from your first marriage. *Your marriage*, Cecily! Oh do wake up a little!'

Cecily opened her eyes, then, her head swaying.

'I am awake. . . .'

'Your father gave you a husband, my dear, when you were only five years old—a solemn ceremony. Your fortune from your mother was to buy him a useful alliance. But he sought to better himself sooner by political means —and then the marriage was useless to him, obnoxious to the other parties . . . Such ceremonies, you know well, are binding. They cannot be set aside unless the church consents. And so you are bound to your husband, Cecily . . . Do you hear me? He cannot marry you to any other without a solemn annulment from His Holiness the Pope . . . Cecily?'

Cecily's eyes were now half closed. She could just see her aunt's face, and by its expression Dame Elizabeth was shouting out in rage and frustration . . . Cecily could not reply. She was already slipping giddily into the crowded darkness she knew so well, where the dark-bearded man was smiling as always, and she was a child seated on his knee. The light from a high coloured window was caught by the jewel in his ear. She had put out her hand to touch his doublet. The padding in the folds was soft and fat, but the gold thread worked into a design of lines and lozenges felt harsh under her fingers, and she drew them away, curling her hand into a fist. She looked up into the face of the grey-beard in his purple gown, who stood close by, and watched him nodding his head. There was music and the room seemed full of people she could not see.

A woman whose face she did not at first distinguish swept her up from the lap of the dark-bearded man and held her, crooning, 'My bird! My pretty bird! My poor bird! Your wings are to be clipped already!' This was her mother, in a tawny gown with jewels like a collar round her throat. A fine light veil floated from her tall head-dress and the hem of her gown was deeply braided with rich embroidery.

'Set her down,' a man's voice said. 'She is not a baby now.' And that was her father.

Even now, lying in her bed, chasing the images through her memory, in and out of a half-sleep, Cecily drew herself together at the tone—the voice lighter than she knew it, but the command the same, and the coldness. This was her wedding day, which none had told her of since; which she was too young to understand at the time; whose image had remained to her in the vague shape of an unresolved dream.

Her mother set the child on her feet and she stood in the centre of the watching circle, the focus of all eyes, not not knowing why—but pleased to be so and smiling prettily if uncertainly to make them smile and nod in

return. There could not be any apprehension in so young
a creature—the fear was the experience of the grown
Cecily, for whom the pictures unfolded as they had never
done before, full of sound and detail and as brightly
coloured as the margins of her aunt's great books from
which she had tried to read.

The crowded room was hot. The women fanned themselves and there was sweat on the men's faces. Only two
were bearded. Some wore long gowns and some short,
and their shoes with toes upcurling, some chained to the
knee, made the small Cecily shrill with laughter.

'Hush!' someone said. 'Little wives are to be quiet and
gentle.'

Then there was a sudden jostling and shifting, for
outside a voice had cried that the Archbishop was riding
into the courtyard. . . .

When they were in the chapel there seemed fewer
people and it was easier to breathe. Now her father held
Cecily by the hand—and she saw it was he who wore a
dark beard and an ear jewel, which was why she had failed
in the past to recognise him—she remembered him always
clean shaven. Had he shaved off his beard, perhaps, with
his Lancastrian loyalties?

The Archbishop, a tall broad man, spoke to her quite
long and earnestly, and only the prettiness of his purple
cap kept her attention fixed. Perhaps he was telling her
not to be afraid, that after the ceremony she should go
home with her mother and her father, and remain with
them until she was old enough to be sent as a wife to her
husband's home . . . Now the gay music had changed
and was solemn, the voices of young boys soared to the
chapel roof. There was linen and lace and the Archbishop
wore a magnificent cope gold-embroidered on every inch.
The little girl looked at the ground and feared to raise her
eyes, for she was growing tired and everyone seemed far

away from her, busy about affairs that depended on her but did not concern her. Her gaze at ground level ran about the feet of the gathering as dartingly and uncertainly as a mouse; then rested on the shoes of the boy on the Archbishop's other hand.

Impatience seized the grown Cecily, wrestling half conscious with pictures that came so fast and changed so ruthlessly that she seemed to hear herself cry out. She struggled to wake, yet knew that she might wake too soon. With his shoes of tan doeskin the boy wore saffron hose. Over a white shirt he wore a short doublet of gold damask, trimmed with narrow fur and gold-belted, and a gold chain round his neck.

Her father stirred behind her, answering some word from the Archbishop. She moved forward as he told her. The boy moved forward, too. The two grown men, the fathers, each took his child's hand and laid it in the hand of the other. Both hands were warm and a little sticky, and both children seemed uncertain about this hand-taking and tried to sheer away. But first the fathers held them, and then the Archbishop put his hand over all and held them firmly together. Under this pile of hands the smallest wriggled and winced against the pressure of bones and muscles and the hard fierce edges of rings. At last, pinched beyond endurance, the girl shrieked and began to cry.

Although this caused a discreet tumult, it was not of disapproval. The men murmured together and smothered laughs, while the women sighed and exclaimed. It was right and seemly that a bride should weep . . . Bless the little creature, she was a woman already in her submissive sadness! The Archbishop released the hands just in time or the bride would have struck out in pain and fright.

They were leaving the chapel. Talk burst out among the adults and the two children seemed forgotten as congratu-

lations passed from father to father, as the mothers
embraced, as the contracts drawn by lawyers were duly
signed and sealed. The boy and the girl were recollected,
then, for they had each to make their mark on the
parchments.

'Salute your bride, boy,' his father ordered, to the
loud laughter of the company. 'Kiss her now, for you
must wait many a long year before you may see her again.'

His father holding him by the shoulders, thrusting
him forward, the boy approached. As he advanced
he stretched his thin neck nervously, kissed her quickly
between the eyes, and flinched back. Even though she
would not look at him, Cecily felt that wincing away. The
patter of amusement from the crowded room made her
flush violently and clench her hands together. . . .

As always at this moment in the dream she began to
struggle—either to wake, and know herself safe—or to
dream on and see more. Her struggles woke her for an
instant and she cried out wildly, for all she was aware of
was her father's face that seemed stooped above her . . .
Immediately, she began to sink back again. This time her
sleep was absolute, so still, so deep that she seemed hardly
to breathe.

Towards morning, Cecily stirred. Opening her eyes
with difficulty she saw that the bed curtains had been
pulled back. Her aunt had no doubt come in the night to
see how she was. The room was empty now, and Meg
must have taken Davy to another bed, for his own in the
corner by the door had not been slept in.

'Lewis must know,' murmured Cecily. But it was
impossible to recall what it was she needed to tell him.
She was so fuddled she could not order her thoughts at
all. Was it that Giles had come? She did remember that.
Or something that her aunt had said to her—she had

talked a lot, but what had it been about? Or perhaps there had been something in her dream that she needed to confide . . . if she could recall at the moment what the dream had been about. Yet Lewis must know, Lewis must be found—she would surely know when she saw him what it was she had to say.

She fumbled her way out of bed, her head swimming so that she had to catch hold of the curtains. Once, between the bed and the chest from which she had picked up her clothes, she fell; but the bundle she carried muffled the sound of the fall.

One thing her muddled brain did tell her—that soon the household would be stirring. Her aunt would surely come again to see if she were waking. It was growing light very fast, and Goody Ann would be jangling the bell to bring them all tumbling and yawning down the narrow stair from the big room under the rafters. If she was to go, she must go now.

In the first light, then, the birds now stirring, Cecily left Mantlemass. The bolts on the big studded door might have troubled her, but in spite of her groping, half numbed fingers they slid as though buttered, and there was no creaking of the heavy hinges as she slipped outside.

The air was sharp, there was frost on the ground as well as a cuckoo calling in the distance. The forest was utterly still, waiting to take breath and begin the day, and she paused, looking out over wood and heathland, afraid of the mystery of the place yet longing to find shelter there. Then she picked up her skirt and went stumbling away from the house, down the narrow path towards the river. She slipped on the stepping stones and her shoes filled with water. With great difficulty she pulled herself up the far bank, but the effort exhausted her, and she fell to her knees, then toppled forward and lay with her cheek against the ground, longing to sleep again. But

10

she was much too near home. She dragged herself up and
continued on her way, and now she was seeking a hiding
place. Ahead of her there was an expanse of scrub, gorse
and bramble and holly matted into an inviting shelter.
She crawled in, rather as Davy had done that first day of
the snow, and this time the intense drowsiness won and
she slept again.

When Cecily next woke her head was entirely, almost
frighteningly clear. She remembered Giles, her father's
plans, the dream of the marriage and why she must find
Lewis. She knew that because the drink, which should
have been soothing, had been like a blow on the head,
Dame Elizabeth had been unable to finish her tale. There
was more. Everything that had happened since she came
to Mantlemass began to fall into place. Her aunt's
sympathy, the promises she had made of happiness, of
giving back what had been taken away. Once she had said
There was a move made in this game that was never revoked;
and had claimed to have come to Mantlemass because she
knew who her neighbours were; with something like
triumph she had cried out, 'Answer me truly. Is he—
young Mallory—is he indeed your dearest friend?'
Through Cecily's happiness, she had claimed, she would
be able to square her account with her brother; but she
had added, truly, that she might still fail . . . .

Cecily left her shelter. Now her feet were firm under
her, her heart thudding, her thoughts racing. She knew
she had seen the emblem sharp and clear in the last
moments of her dream, not, as it had seemed on a
previous occasion, as a promise for the future—but as a
promise continuing from the past.

Now indeed she knew what it was she had to say to
Lewis Mallory.

It was *Can you remember*?

10
Forest

Lewis that night had had no fevered dreams as Cecily had done. Instead, he had not slept at all, but had sat on his bed or walked the floor, trying to persuade himself that she would understand why, after all, he had not sought the help of Sir James. The suggestion that the priest should solve their problems by marrying them had been easily made. While they were together anything seemed possible. But reason had to prevail. Cecily would surely see as he did how hard a choice this would offer Sir James. His affections, his sympathies were with them —the young—but his responsibility could only be to their elders. He could not in conscience do as he was asked. In the darkness and quiet of midnight this was overwhelmingly clear to Lewis and he was quite bowed down by the difficulties of the situation. Cecily's conviction that her aunt would help them appeared to him too fantastic for belief. This was not necessarily because he had come to mistrust her motives, but because he could not easily imagine how any woman, even one as bold as Dame Elizabeth, would be able to overcome the authority of a father. He knew because his cousin had told him how his own mother had tried to prevail and keep her son—but what good had that done him? Women were simply not able to overrule such circumstances.

It seemed to Lewis, increasingly despairing as the night plodded over, that their only hope lay in flight. If they were to hope for any happiness together, then they must leave the forest and go very far away, and struggle to make their own way in the world. This would demand great courage. If he was to ask it of her, then he must make sure she was aware what the consequences would be if they were overtaken. She would be bound to suffer for her disgrace, while him they would certainly kill.

The morning did not bring Lewis any great comfort. When they next met, which would surely be today, he would have to tell Cecily the conclusions he had come to, such as they were, and how, if they were to be secretly married, it could not be by Sir James; he greatly feared her distress. He set about his work that morning with a dogged kind of energy, for the sooner he was finished with it, the sooner he would be free to seek her. He was grooming his own Iris, whom no one else must handle, when Nicholas Forge rode into the yard.

Lewis left Iris and took the visitor's horse. 'When did you return from London?' he asked.

'Last evening before dusk. I have your cousin's business to discuss.'

'He's indoors. His sister is in a tantrum and only he can calm her. Go to him—I'll see to the bay.'

'I will tell you this before I go,' Nicholas said. 'I was not the only man to ride to Mantlemass last night. The other was a servant of Sir Thomas Jolland.'

He might almost as well have said at once that all plans were in vain. The shock of the news was so great that for a second Lewis could not reply. 'What did he want?' he said at last. 'Where is Sir Thomas, then?'

'I heard in London he had quit France on a journey. He's not so many miles from here, I'd say—he sent his man to fetch the young lady to him.'

'To fetch her . . . ?'

'Well, this I judged to be his purpose. I could not eavesdrop the whole conversation. But it seemed Dame Elizabeth would not discuss the matter. The fellow was sent away. But he will come again, she says.' Nicholas looked at Lewis in a questioning way, as though uncertain how much he should say. 'Next time, she says, he will not come alone.'

'Thank you for your confidence,' Lewis said, and turned away, because he was ashamed of what must be in his face for all to see. He went to the stable and, abandoning Iris, began to saddle up Ebony. As he led the stallion out, his cousin Orlebar came into the yard from the house, and greeted Nicholas Forge, still dallying and looking uneasily after Lewis.

'Where are you going?' Roger Orlebar asked, seeing the horse saddled.

'To Mantlemass.'

'Not now. I need you. Master Forge and I have matters to discuss and you shall hear them.'

'I have had bad news. I must go.'

'Bad news? And you must go to Mantlemass?' He looked at Nicholas. 'What now?'

'Before I left the house last night a servant of Sir Thomas Jolland was there.'

'And what of that?' Roger Orlebar cried. 'I would be happier if I had never heard the name Jolland!'

'I mean to change it,' Lewis said, growing paler and prouder and more foolishly bold with every minute.

'You mean *what*? Now God be my witness, Lewis— you cannot have her! I have tried to tell you this, but I see I should have been a sight more direct. I have only had one confidence, ever, from Dame Elizabeth. But it was this: that the girl was contracted in marriage by her father when she was barely out of the cradle. If it weren't for political troubles she'd have had her own household by now. There. Now you have it.'

Lewis laughed.

'Are you determined not to believe me? You know well that Sir Thomas lost your father's friendship and respect when he turned traitor to Lancaster. The same act, so Dame Elizabeth says, lost him his son-in-law. But the marriage was made and has not been undone. No doubt it will be, fast enough, when he finds another husband who'll be useful to him . . . Well now you will see why I have been amazed at her frivolity in letting you two have so much freedom.'

'I think you must be lying, sir,' Lewis said. He spoke with difficulty for his teeth seemed to be chattering and he could not get his tongue round the words. 'She never spoke of it. . . .'

'How should she, poor child? She was a babe, I tell you—she would not even remember. How much do you remember of your time before you came here—but you were older than she must have been at that time.'

'I forgot through necessity, cousin.' He turned and put his foot in the stirrup.

'Lewis! You are to stay here with me!'

'I must speak with her!' shouted Lewis, throwing himself into the saddle and moving off fast before he had even found his second stirrup.

'You poor young fool!' Roger Orlebar bellowed after him, deeply distressed. 'Why—why could you not be warned in time?'

Cecily pushed her way through the scrub and ran down the slope towards the wider track that led one way to Ghylls Hatch, the other towards the weaver's cottage. Then she heard a sound and slid behind a tree to watch.

There were two riders, mounted on a roan and a chestnut, making their way in her direction. They moved uncertainly, pausing and pointing one way or another, consulting together, perhaps quarrelling for she could hear a rise in their voices. They were strangers to the forest, a man and a woman.

Neither was a stranger to Cecily, however. The man was Giles. The woman was Alys.

Cecily shrank in her hiding place, then stepping back a pace or two, let the neighbouring bushes swallow her. She watched the pair as they picked their way with distaste and obvious unease along a boggy edge and reached the open track. They halted no more than ten yards from her.

'I came to the place the other way last night,' Giles was saying. 'There was a fellow ahead of me—I followed his lead. How was I to know I should be forced to ride the same way again?'

'You might have known it. Men! Did you think—you and Sir Thomas—that such a woman as Dame Elizabeth would hand the girl over with no fuss?'

'There was no reason to think otherwise.'

'What fools!' Alys cried impatiently. 'I should have been with you.'

'Which way now, then?' Giles asked, 'Since you know all that should be done—which way do we turn?'

'I know nothing of the way,' snapped Alys. 'I only know he bade us make great haste. If we don't fetch her to him soon, he'll come after her himself.'

'I pray he may like her when he gets her. Your pretty creature looks as rough as a milkmaid. She's found her tongue, too, and it's a sharp one.'

'So you say—so you say. But I know her well. She's soft and easy and her tempers are only childish. I have always been able to show her what's best for her own good. I shall do so again.'

Cecily's fingers curled and uncurled. So Alys had been sent to persuade her she should return to her loving father—to paint pretty pictures, no doubt, of the joys of marriage and the glories of a high situation among the French nobility. She might even, Cecily thought, willing to believe in any treachery now, tell her that this was the very suitor they two had so often spoken of, the peerless knight for whom she had been saved, whose perfection demanded equal perfection in his bride . . . Had Alys known all along, Cecily wondered, that before any marriage could take place that earlier ceremony must be declared officially null and void?

'The sun's to our left, Alys. I think we should turn north.'

'Does no one live in these outlandish parts, to tell us the way?'

'See for yourself,' said Giles, then changed his tone. 'No, wait—there's a child coming this way. See him? If he can talk at all, and God knows only savages could exist here, he may at least know the name Mantlemass.'

Cecily peered anxiously through the bushes. Davy was coming along the track. He had not yet seen the riders. He was jogging along and she could hear him mumbling to himself. Was he looking for her—or making off about his secret affairs?

'You there—boy!' called Giles.

Davy stopped in his tracks and turned tail. But when Giles bellowed after him he paused, as usual responding to harshness as he never did to kindness.

'Come here and answer me civilly,' Giles ordered.

Davy stood shuffling his feet and ready to bolt. Giles nudged his horse up and the boy took a pace backwards, but Alys also moved her mount swiftly and headed him off. He stood between the two of them, staring up in panic at the strange faces. He was not accustomed to seeing anyone but those he knew, and Cecily was hard pressed not to go to his rescue.

'Which way for Mantlemass?' asked Alys.

Davy was very small, standing there by the horses, both of which by chance were tall and rather raking beasts. He looked around him as if judging the best way to escape. As he did so, he glanced under the belly of the roan towards the inviting scrub. He looked directly into Cecily's face.

His expression was always guarded, but it lightened so pleasingly that at any other moment she would have rejoiced at this proof of his concern. She slid her hand towards her face, terrified of making any sharp movement, and laid her finger on her lips, slightly shaking her head. It was not much of a sign to give a child of doubtful intelligence. If he failed her there would be nothing for it but instant flight. Although by now she knew her way about the tracks, she would have to plunge into the undergrowth if she was to escape pursuers on horseback, and there was no doubt at all that she would very soon be lost. She stared at Davy, willing him to understand, and he stared back, while Giles and Alys bullied and wheedled above his head.

'Which is the track for Mantlemass? Are you dumb, you young lout?'

'We are friends of the pretty lady, child. Can you tell us where she lives?'

Davy frowned. It was painful to watch him thinking. It was as though his brain began to stir for the very first time—and as though the sensation was too strange to be enjoyable.

At last, very slowly, he withdrew his glance in a sliding manner from Cecily, turning his shoulder to her. He raised his arm and pointed down a side path that led nowhere of the least interest to the riders, but through much delaying mud and roughness eventually to the iron workings of Master Urry.

'There! Good child!' cried Alys. 'Toss him half a farthing, Giles.'

'I've no time to fumble for rewards. And half a farthing's a fortune to an idiot's child. Besides—how do I know to trust him?' He cracked his whip, and then sent the leash curling around Davy's ankles. 'You shall show us the way. On with you, now, or I'll whip you to a better pace!'

With no cry of protest, with no glance for help, Davy ran ahead of the horses, leading them firmly in the direction he had chosen. Soon they were out of sight. Cecily stayed where she was, uncertain where to move next and worried about Davy, lest he should suffer for his deception. Yet she felt fairly confident that whatever his inability to express himself, he had a native sense that would take care of him.

She moved cautiously from the shelter of the bushes. Now her course was not so easy. If she went by the obvious route to Ghylls Hatch she must follow a part of the way behind the riders. This thought made her uneasy, for what if they suddenly turned back the way they had come? If they found her alone they would not ask her aunt's leave to take her, that was sure. She was sturdier than she used to be, but she was still small and light and could easily be carried away against her will. This threat filled her with a wild panic, for the thought that she might still lose what she had almost gained was not to be endured. She took to her heels and ran on the path that linked with the one leading near the weaver's cottage, and so in a broad loop back at last to Ghylls Hatch.

The sun was now shining strongly, the sky was clear and nothing remained of the early morning's chill. The forest burgeoned as she looked at it, the trees increasingly green, the bluebells deepening in colour, the pale wood sorrel rioting with violets both white and blue—and all seeming to grow around and over her, threatening almost to imprison her. The ground that sloped away to the river running in its valley below the weaver's cottage seemed to carry her with it, helping her along. Outside his cottage she saw the weaver seated and milking a black-and-white goat. At the same moment she felt a drumming in the soles of her feet and knew that within seconds she would be overtaken by a galloping horse. There was no scrub here to shelter her, and the trees were tall. She threw herself down to the river and scrambled through the water and up the far bank. The weaver looked up, but did not speak, and without any more than a glance she ran straight on into his cottage. She stood inside the doorway and peered out.

It was red-bearded Henty who shot into view below. He pulled up short when he saw the weaver and shouted up to him.

'Has anyone passed? Dame Elizabeth is seeking her niece. Has she been by here, weaver? Would you have seen her if she had?'

'I should've seen her, surely,' replied the weaver. 'Get off with you now, mus' Henty—you're fritting poor Nanny.'

'Oh be hanged to poor Nanny! The girl's vanished herself and must be found.'

'Justly so,' agreed the weaver. 'And good-day to you.'

He watched Henty out of sight, then stripped the last drops of milk into the pail, and slapped Nanny off to her grazing. He came into the cottage, pail in one hand, stool in the other. 'Are you there, my maid?' he asked softly.

She was leaning against the wall and answered him faintly, out of breath from leaping up the bank.

'You look fairly jawled-out,' he said. 'Wait till I find a dipper and I'll hand you some milk.'

Even then, Cecily smiled at the words. She accepted the warm, cheesy milk and was glad of it. She had eaten no supper last night and the drink her aunt had given her was poor preparation for a day's running through the forest.

'Mus' Henty goes seeking you,' the weaver said. 'Will you get home to Mantlemass?'

'No,' said Cecily. 'For it is not only he who seeks me and I will go nowhere and speak to no one till I have found Lewis Mallory. So if he should come this way, weaver, tell him I am gone through the forest to his home and will wait for him there. And tell him there has never been anything in his life or mine so necessary as that we should speak together at once. Tell him.'

'What has come to you?' he asked.

'The best,' she said. 'Or the worst. When I have asked a question—then I shall know. But I have my wits still,' she added, seeing his startled look, and knowing that she did indeed sound a little mad. 'I am bitterly hungry, weaver. Have you some bread?' His hesitation was so fine she was not sure she had seen it. It was only when she had eaten the bread that she realised it might have been his own dinner. 'You have helped me,' she said quickly. 'I shall help you when I can.'

When she had left him she retraced her steps, facing again towards Ghylls Hatch. If Henty was out looking for her there could be others—Nicholas Forge, Tom Bostel, Sim—half a dozen more, and none of them would she trust, lest her father had bought them. She began to run. Above all else in life she needed Lewis. The best or the worst, she had said to Halacre, the weaver. If it was the worst, then she would remember what they had vowed together. She would die, if need be, but she would not live without him.

The forest was increasingly trampled by riding men. Had her father sent an army to seek her? Once she saw Tom Bostel, and once Roger Orlebar—she almost called to him. But there were many strangers, and it was some time before she remembered that the ordinary business of the forest remained, and not all these riders sought her, but went, rather, about their concerns—with the iron workings, or the mill, or the weaver, or with the business of ordering charcoal, inspecting timber, or even poaching game.

This realisation did little for Cecily. She was deathly tired and this caused her increasing panic. Now she felt as her aunt's coneys must feel when, driven by barking and snapping from the warrens, they found themselves tangling in the wicked nets, and turned and twisted and screamed in vain. She began to run wildly, to mistake the tracks. She slid out of sight in clumps of seedling birch, and flung herself down in concealing hollows, though sometimes she was running from nothing but her own imagination and strained eyes. She was forever coming full circle. Her hair was in her eyes, her shoes sopping from scrambling through the many little rivers. The hem

of her dress, soaked and heavy, slapped against her ankles
—she had lost all sense of direction, and even the sun,
being directly overhead, could not help her. She stopped
to think, hunching her shoulders in fear, clenching her
muscles and trembling. Meg had said the forest would not
let her go, and perhaps she had been right. Perhaps there
was nothing more than to drop down and die here in the
tangle of undergrowth, taking with her her hopes and her
love, and never knowing what Lewis would have answered
to the question she had had no chance to ask him.

She lay still where fatigue had dropped her, thinking
of all this, and the sun declined and the trees made some
sort of dial for her to read if she could. But all she learnt
was that Mantlemass, Ghylls Hatch, the weaver's
cottage, the meeting place by the pool were all somewhere
behind her—no finger pointed the way she should take
now. She pulled herself to her feet, trying to feel angry
with her own stupidity in getting so completely lost,
rather than helpless and afraid. She pushed on through a
copse of young birch tangled with newly sprouting
brambles. Some sort of clearing was ahead of her, with a
tumbledown hovel huddled into the curve of the trees.
It looked like many charcoal burners' cottages she had
seen, and because she feared the darkness and the roughness of the burners, she faltered. The place was shabby
with stamped-out fires, a dilapidated faggot stack, a
broken well-head from which hung a battered wooden
bucket. The windows of the hovel were stuffed with
rags and the stench of poverty defeated even the clean
forest air. It was the meanest place Cecily had ever seen,
and instinctively she turned from it. But there was a
woman in a tattered brown dress standing by the door
looking at her. Peering round her skirt was a very small
boy, and cropping the grass close at hand was a fine grey
mare with flowing mane and tail.

The woman was Joan; the boy was her son Davy; the mare was Zephyr. . . .

Davy ran to Cecily, then paused. For a second, torn and weary as she was, he must have wondered if she was another stranger.

'Davy, Davy . . . ' she said, her voice faint with fatigue. She looked at his mother. 'Joan—is it you?'

'And is it you, I might wonder! What a sight to be sure! I got turned off by that fellow Timothy from Orlebars. But I left him shy of a mount. Yon's your Zephyr.'

'I see it is.'

'You're looked for,' Joan said, her manner as ugly and defiant as ever. 'But if they saw you they might not want you. Where's my lady now? There's Mantlemass men and strangers—there's a fine straight man, as bold as a nobleman—all looking for you. Why's that?'

'Bold as a nobleman . . . My father's here, then. He sent for me. But I will not go . . . May I drink from the well?'

'You've need of more than well water, by the looks of you . . . Come indoors. Here's where my mam lives, and I come back to her, and Davy come back to me. Did you hear of Goody Luke? A wise woman, she is. That's my mam. She'll help you.'

Cecily hesitated. Though she was too tired to be troubled by the squalor of the place, she was uncertain if Joan was to be trusted any more than the next one. Perhaps she had spoken with the fine straight man, as bold as a nobleman. . . .

'Take her hand, Davy,' Joan said.

'I wondered where he went for so long . . . ' Cecily murmured. Her head swam and she caught at Davy as though he was big enough to support her.

'Do I have to say it loud?' cried Joan angrily. 'You done well for my boy. What could I do but well for you? Choose, then, and sharp about it. Stay or go?'

'I'll stay,' Cecily said; and let Davy pull her indoors.

Goody Luke was nothing like the crone Cecily had expected. She was twice as handsome as her sullen daughter, with black silky hair and a white skin that made her look like some beautiful wicked fairy. She took Cecily's chin in her hand and tilted up her face, and then pulled down her lower eyelids, making sounds of increasing disapproval.

'Black as sloes,' she said. 'That's over-much of fox-glove. Who give you the drink, lady dear?'

'Meg made it as she was told to—too strong, my aunt said. It made me dream and it made me sleep—and I think my head's still swimming with it.'

'Bring a mug of poad-milk, Joan. The best for cleansing and lucky we got it for her . . . Drink it slow,' she said, when the mug was in her hands. 'That's the first from the heifer just calved, lady.' She looked Cecily up and down and shook her head. 'There's a dissight! And my Joan tell me you'm so picksome and dainty.'

'How far to Ghylls Hatch?' Cecily asked.

'Too far, I'd say.'

'Then I'll take Zephyr.'

'You'll be out of the saddle and break your neck,' Joan said. 'Rest here. Didn't they tell you anyone running is safe with foresters? Davy boy—go find Lewis Mallory and bring him this way. Run fast, there's a good boy. Run fast! And Davy—' He paused, looking so small it did not seem possible he had the legs to run for miles through the forest. 'Keep hid from strangers, Davy.'

Halfway to Mantlemass, stupefied by what his cousin had told him, Lewis met Meg running wildly. He pulled up Ebony at once, calling to her, shouting to know what was the matter—for it seemed to him that no disaster was too great to fall upon him.

'Oh quickly, quickly!' Meg cried. 'Gone from Mantlemass, she has, and none knows where, and last night there come her father's man to fetch her away—'

'I know that. What are you saying—she's gone from Mantlemass? Have they taken her?'

'If they did—then it was right from her bed—it's not likely. She run out, Lord knows how early—early as dawn and frost on the ground. And soon after, Sir Thomas himself, her own father, come roaring and sworling after her. All through the house he went, with Dame Elizabeth watching—for she knew my young lady was gone. He pulled the very curtains from the beds and flung the covers on the floor. He cursed and roared, and she—the mistress—she cursed back, till Mary and me must cover our ears.'

'Go on—go on!'

'At last he were done with Mantlemass, and he rid off, and he was swearing still and blaspheming. Then my mistress sent every man about the place to get horses and seek through the forest. And I'm sent to Master Orlebar to ask his help, for there's not a man or a lad left at home. Nothing I ever saw were so bad as the mistress crying and sobbing, as none ever thought to see her. Oh Jesu, she say, over and over, find her—find her 'fore he do and carry her away!'

'Go quickly to Ghylls Hatch, Meg. I'll ride on. And Meg—if you have any breath left in your body by then—take word to Sir James.'

'It might be my last living act—but I'll do it,' Meg promised. 'And do you ride fast and strong, for it's you she needs.'

Yes, she does need me, Lewis thought, but not as I am now—cast down and a coward . . . He straightened himself in the saddle. The forest displayed itself before him as he paused a second on the summit west of Mantlemass, uncertain which way to choose. Not yet in full leaf, the fast thickening trees seemed to be as dense as high green walls. The scrub too was filling out in the first strong growth of the year. The open heathland stretched to the south, so pitted and dipping into deep ghylls and twisting combes that it seemed to Lewis then as impenetrable as any other part. Somewhere in that wide wild place Cecily was running or hiding or lying injured and afraid, and the only advantage her friends had over her enemies was their knowledge of the ground. But there were places she might hide where not even the deer ran, and fugitives had been found too late before now.

As Lewis chose his direction, ready to cover every foot of ground if need be, his thoughts were so bleak and cold it might well have been deep winter still. For if her father or her father's people found her, then he must never hope to see her again, even to say goodbye; and if Dame Elizabeth's people found her, since she was already promised and signed away in marriage, the goodbye must still be spoken. And half his anguish was what she must feel when she learnt the truth, for unless she had been told as recently as he had, then he knew she was ignorant of what had taken place so far in her childhood. *She was a babe*, his cousin had said . . . There was no end to the pain of Lewis's thoughts as he rode searching. As the day went on the possibility nagged at him that, lost and stumbling, she might have made her way into fatal bogland; that she might have fallen into one of the many disused mine pits, and broken her neck, or if it was flooded, drowned. Or that, drowsy from snake bite, she was lying hidden and helpless, dying and alone. Often he tethered Ebony and beat about in the undergrowth.

At noon he saw Henty and Bostel, consulting together, weary with riding and with worry. And once he saw a stranger. He, too, was perplexed, pausing baffled at the mouth of a long ride. The man was Sir Thomas Jolland, and Lewis knew him, strangely, because of his daughter's likeness. He was half surprised by the fine proud looks, expecting rather that any man who had been called traitor must of necessity look sly and slinking. For the first time ever in his life, the desire to strike and kill an enemy moved hotly in Lewis; he put his hand on his knife and loosened it in its sheath, and waited. But Sir Thomas saved him his decision by moving off impatiently, and soon he had disappeared among the trees.

From then on, getting deeper and deeper into the forest, Lewis saw none but charcoal burners and the like who, when he asked, knew nothing. It was their nature to know nothing, to hide the fugitive. But he knew they would have told him what they could; he was a forester as they were and many of them must have seen him about the forest with Cecily, riding side by side and hand in hand.

At last, in the very early evening, he rode once more to their meeting place by the pool. She was not there. But Davy came running to meet him.

11
The Lark and the Laurel

It was dusky enough in Goody Luke's cottage even when
the sun was bright. Now that evening had almost come
the place was full of shadows, and with only a rushlight
to help him Lewis had thought at first that he would not
be able to read Cecily's face. He was uncertain what he
expected to find there. There must be fear at her father's
return, but he had no means of knowing whether it was
he who must break to her the bitter news his cousin
had given him that morning. He dreaded what it might
do to her. Lesser disasters had made both men and women
lose their wits. He had told himself that he must renounce
her in the first instant of their meeting—must resist the
impulse to hold and comfort her and must never embrace

her again. For even if he was ready to sacrifice his own hope of heaven, he would not sacrifice hers . . . All this he had thought as he rode as fast as he could, with a sleepy Davy perched on the saddle in front of him and likely to roll off unless he were securely held. He had thought far and deep into the future, learning minute by minute how much he must lose—not least the pleasant image of holding his own son before him as he now held Davy.

But the instant Lewis came through the door of that dim, rank hovel, Cecily sprang up and threw herself into his arms, kissing and caressing him and even laughing with relief and delight to see him. He was powerless, then. His resolves fled utterly and they clung together in comfort and warmth—so that immediately it had seemed impossible that they could ever be parted.

'You were about seven or eight years old,' Cecily was murmuring, as he kissed her cheek where the brambles had torn it. 'Lewis—listen to me. Do you remember the Archbishop?'

For a second he thought all his fears had been justified—the shock of this business had sent her out of her mind.

'What archbishop, love?'

'Think back. Please, please—think back, think hard. You told me once you were with your father in France. . . .'

'I thought it was so—my cousin told me it was so. But I have forgotten.'

'Oh Lewis—pray think—think. Was there not some day when you dressed in your best?'

'Well—I would suppose so. The king was there. They must have kept some state. But you know I have forgotten those times. I never think of my parents or my home—you know that. I will not do so. There is a great wall raised up between then and now—I have told you this.'

'Dearest Lewis,' she said, 'for both our sakes, tear
down the wall. For when I was in France there was just
such a day for me. I was dressed in a stiff white gown—
my wedding gown, Lewis—it was my marriage day.
No—don't move away from me but hold me hard. I was
five years old . . . .'

'My cousin told me. This morning, he told me. I
thought I felt my heart break. But you—you seem hardly
to care.'

'Oh Lewis—remember! You must remember! Were
you not there, too? In a gold doublet and saffron hose and
shoes well pointed? You think I am mad but I am truly
sane—perhaps as never before. Now my father comes
with news that he has chosen me a new husband, one
with a high connection in the church who will set about
the annulment of that older contract. But it must be
confirmed—not broken. Remember—oh please, remember! Think of all that has been said and done—think of
my aunt and her mysteries—of your father casting you
away. Was it not because a useful marriage had become a
dangerous one—because my father had forsworn his
allegiance and found himself betterment another way?'

She was steady as a rock now, her voice low and full of
a passionate excitement. It was he who shivered and
sweated.

'If I could remember,' he said, 'what should it be?'

'You are afraid to say it!' she cried. 'Oh you coward,
Lewis Mallory! You would remember that the day I
was wed, when the ceremony was done, your father
pushed you towards me and told you to kiss your bride . . .
Yes, Lewis—yes! You were the bridegroom! His hands
were on your shoulders and I saw the ring. I saw it—the
lark and the laurel engraved there in a red-brown stone.'

His hand moved to his throat and he pulled out his ring
on its leather thong. 'How do you remember so much?'

'I have never forgotten—I have never quite forgotten. It has always been a half-dream—'

'Ah,' he said, 'but a dream none the less. And a sweet dream, Cecily . . . But too good, too easy . . . Oh God, if I could remember! You seem so sure. If you are right— then are we married? Safe?'

'When my father knows we have found one another— then, yes—surely, we are safe.'

'We must be certain.'

'Let my aunt tell us. Last night she would have told me, but I slept too soon . . . That's another story . . . If I had known what I was doing I might not have left Mantlemass this morning. When I came to my senses I had to see you before anything else in the world . . . I am sorry I have troubled you so.'

'Your father was at Mantlemass. As well you left. . . .'

'We'll go to my aunt now. I am certain what she will tell us. I am sure and certain. I have seen it all.'

'But a dream, Cecily—you said it was a dream.'

'I call it a dream. Remember, Lewis—remember! Dreams are not shared—only realities.'

All this time Joan and her mother and Davy had remained outside, but now Joan came quickly indoors to say that Sir James was crossing the clearing to the cottage door.

'I'll send him packing, if that's what you tell me to. The priest's no friend of mine.'

Lewis was at the door before she had finished. Sir James wore his cassock tucked into his belt and his bare legs showed how far and how deep he had ranged about the forest that day.

'You must leave here,' he said at once, not pausing for a greeting. 'Your father, my child—surely a most fierce determined man. He's going from cottage to cottage, threatening to burn the thatches about their heads.

There's two foresters in the river already and another with
a broken head. Come now—you must come with me. If
need be we'll get you into sanctuary in the palace chapel.
He dare not touch you there.'

Lewis took Cecily's hand and led her quickly outside.
He put her up on Ebony and mounted behind her. 'Go
with your mother and the boy into the forest, Joan,' he
said. 'Let him find the place empty . . . Father—take the
grey. She and Ebony are well matched. The saddle, Joan!'

It was slung over the branch of a tree and between them
Joan and the priest dragged it down and he was mounted
almost as soon as Lewis had settled Cecily in comfort.

'We'll need to go by the causeway,' Lewis said. 'We've
two good horses and they'll carry us with no panic. But
that way we must go, for sure.'

'You know best, my son.' The priest paused, looking
down at Joan. 'My good girl—' he began, and she
laughed, for it was not the way she was usually addressed,
least of all by a churchman. 'I pray you,' he said, flushing,
'go to Dame Elizabeth and tell her where her niece will
be.'

'I'll do it for her,' Joan said, jerking her head at Cecily,
'and that means I'll be doing it for Davy.'

'God bless you,' he said firmly, defying her to reject
the words. Turning Zephyr's head then, he followed at
once after Lewis.

Between the high ground that swept strongly east and
west, where Mantlemass and Ghylls Hatch stood at
several miles distance, the forest swooped down towards
a broad bottom. The river running there crossed many
miles before sinking down and finding its own level,
exchanging as it did so its clear running breadth with
many falls, for a wide area of bog and marshland. Here
at one point it broadened into a lake, the surface so weed-

covered that it looked from above to be part of the valley
floor. Local lore declared this lake to be bottomless, and
Lewis could remember when Jenufer had frightened him
with tales of a great serpent living in its depths. He had
never quite outgrown a superstitious fear of the place,
and he would go a long way round at any time to avoid
picking a path along the sagging causeway, built so long
ago that time had almost worn it away. To reach the palace
chapel on the far ridge, however, in the quickest possible
time, the obvious route ran here. Lewis had known
horses refuse the causeway, but he was sure of Ebony
and Zephyr—Ebony would carry him anywhere, and
Zephyr would follow.

The urgency and speed of their departure from Joan's
cottage had put an end to words. Lewis rode silently, his
mind whirling. Cecily, in her torn and dirty dress, her
face scratched, her hair tangled with bits of briar, leant
warmly against him clutching the horse's mane. He could
scarcely see her face and had indeed little opportunity to
look at her, for his eyes were on the road ahead, and on
the horizon, north and south, where an enemy might
appear. Yet he knew without seeing it that danger had not
taken the strange contentment from her features. For him,
in spite of all she had said, the doubt and the puzzlement
and the fear of bitter sorrow remained. She had spoken of
a dream. It was a fatal word. Dreams could be no better
than wishes, he knew that.

They rode warily, even before they left the copses and
the coverts, not crashing a way through, but steadily
avoiding those places where fallen branches could crack
and splinter, or where overhanging greenery thrust aside
would swish and sigh and sway after they had gone,
marking their passage. At last they emerged from shelter
and faced down the south side of the wide ghyll. The dusk
was flushed with the end of a fine and promising sunset,

so that the slopes with their heather cover just making new dark leafage were plum purple, broken with black peat scars and the livid green of coarse tufty marsh grasses. There were still some lingering patches of dead bracken, which in this light glowed iron-red. Since it was still spring, the weeds that covered the bottomless lake were not entirely grown, and the exposed stretches of water gave back the curiously tinted sky. Wisps of mist were combed over the bog.

It was only now that Cecily stirred and asked how far— how far to safety?

'Three or four miles. But on the causeway we must be patient. It is not a ride to make at speed.'

'I see where it runs—along the water's edge. Is that the way?'

'Yes.'

'It is very narrow.'

'So is a horse's tread,' said Lewis, unwilling to admit that for almost three hundred paces the causeway ran with fathomless water on one side and deep bog on the other. He had once asked the priest how the causeway came there at all, and he had said that perhaps men even more ancient than the Romans had tried to drain the marsh and cultivate the rich soil. So to the strangeness of the place there seemed to be added the ghosts of men long gone—their bodies, perhaps, lying quiet still in the bog.

Cecily looked back across Lewis's shoulder. Sir James was riding some four lengths behind. In the increasing dark she could not see his face clearly, but his presence gave her reassurance. She wondered if Joan would truly go to Mantlemass, and believed that she would. Perhaps already Dame Elizabeth was calling for Farden and setting out towards the palace. Cecily looked up the valley towards the swoop of the skyline. Almost unconsciously she looked for her aunt—and immediately seemed to see

her. There was a horse, small in the distance yet so sharp
against the skyline that it was possible to see a woman's
skirt blowing against its flank.

'My aunt is coming, Lewis.'

'Your aunt? No—she will not come this way.' Lewis
looked back in his turn, and then so did the priest.

'There are two,' he shouted. 'A man and a woman.'

'Giles and Alys,' said Cecily, tightening her hold.
'We must go faster!'

They were still far away, but they would see as clearly
as they were seen in this curious light. The final up-
flushing of the sunset seemed to sharpen all the forest
contours and the two distant riders poured themselves
over the horizon and came fast on the sloping track
towards the bottom of the ghyll. Their flight was aided
and speeded by the lie of the land, but those ahead had
slowed to a delicate walk as they took the head of the
causeway. The distance between the two parties was like
a snake swallowing its tail.

'They are bound to check,' Lewis said. 'They cannot
take you here, be sure of that.'

'But they might drown us all!'

'Yes. They might do that!'

'Take care!' she cried, pressing against him.

He laughed. 'Leave me some breath, then.' He laid
his cheek briefly against her hair. 'No parting without
meeting,' he said, so quietly that he could not tell if she
heard. 'At least we have that comfort.'

By now Ebony was halfway across, Zephyr well up
behind. The pursuers seemed to fly down the last incline.
Now they in their turn had reached the causeway. But
the first horse refused. It reared, squealing, and both
Lewis and the priest looked back, and simultaneously
laid a hand each on the neck of his own horse. For Ebony
and Zephyr had flattened their ears at the noise behind

them. Zephyr tossed her head and snorted, her nostrils widening.

Between quieting Ebony, unused in any case to a double load, and glancing back constantly to see how the pursuit went, Lewis was much occupied. He was concerned, too, for Zephyr. The priest was a robust rider, but the grey was such a sensitive creature she might in emergency resent a stranger's hands and kick up her heels. Now both the pursuing horses had been forced by their riders on to the causeway. Ebony needed only twenty or so paces to reach firm ground, but Lewis dared not hurry him.

Sir James called, 'They're moving up! They are riding it too fast—they'll kill the lot of us!'

At the same moment there was a flurry behind. The leading horse, ridden by Giles, had picked up a defiant speed and could not be held. He struggled to check the creature, whose hindquarters dipped perilously as one hoof struck on the moss-grown stone on which the causeway was founded. There was a great sound of striking, struggling hoofs. Giles shouted, and behind him Alys gave a thin, high scream that made Cecily bury her head against Lewis's shoulder.

'Don't look round,' he said. He felt Zephyr pressing up behind him and heard her blowing. He heeled Ebony and the horse rose nobly in a great leap over the last stretch and went tearing up the bank over the blessed hard earth.

Lewis reined in, then. He looked back and down. Giles and his mount were in the water, the horse strongly swimming, the man grabbing at its tail. Then, as though the legendary serpent had seized him and dragged him down, the man sank like a stone and did not re-appear. Alys screamed and screamed, her horse on its hind legs and threatening to slay her, too. But somehow it turned, half plunged and recovered, then went fast, fast back up the hillside and far out of sight.

Zephyr, riderless, came at a gallop up the hill, checked at the sight of Ebony and shuddered to a standstill. As he snatched at the rein, Lewis was trembling for his tutor. Then he saw that Sir James was kneeling on the causeway and knew that he was sending a hopeful prayer after the drowned man. The horse had reached dry land and stood for a second, water pouring from its back, reins dangling, stirrups flying, before following after its fellow up the hill.

By the time Sir James had plodded up the hillside Zephyr was quiet and he re-mounted easily enough. No one spoke. They rode on, the priest now leading, and cantering easily over a grassy track they came within minutes to the roofless palace sprawling on its ridge, with the chapel and the priest's lodging as quiet and untroubled as if this evening were an evening like any other.

'Now come safe inside, my dearest children,' the priest said. And he shot the bolts of the great door behind them.

The chapel was very fine. Even in her present state of mind, even in the pale light of the oil lamps Sir James had kindled for them, Cecily saw the colour and the gold, the high roof, the painted glass. She held Lewis's hand tightly, determined that he should not escape her, and it was she who led him after the priest to the altar.

'Father,' said Cecily, making Lewis kneel beside her, but still holding his hand, 'when I was a child I was given in marriage. For all the years of my life I had a dream about this, but only last night my aunt made it clear for me. It is my true conviction that the husband I was promised to then is kneeling beside me now. Pray, Father James, let us be married again, knowing what we do.'

'What do you say to this, Lewis?' Sir James asked his pupil gently. 'Am I to marry you because your Cecily has had a dream?' He was half smiling, half frowning.

'I cannot break the early contract, you know that. If she is wed, then she is wed and there is nothing we can do.'

'I saw the ring,' Cecily insisted, beginning to falter. 'The lark and the laurel that is the Mallory emblem. I saw it, on his father's hand. And I should not have called it a dream, but a memory that has been there always, waiting for me to understand. Give me the ring, Lewis. Put it on my finger and put your hand on mine. And even if he will not bless us, I will swear to be faithful only to you.'

She had begun to cry and the tears fell on Lewis's hands as he did as she asked. The ring was huge on her finger, but he held it in place.

'I implore you, Father,' wept Cecily. 'I know this is the truth.'

'Poor children,' he muttered. He put his hand on theirs, unable to resist her tears and wanting only to comfort both of them. And because this was a moment of great concern for him, his grip was hard and painful, the large ring bit into Cecily's finger and she cried out, her fingers fighting under Lewis's. . . .

'Oh God in heaven,' Lewis said very quietly, 'it was the Archbishop, just as you said—in a gold-embroidered cope . . . Your hand was hurt—and you cried. . . .'

Sir James had bolted the big door of the chapel but no one had remembered the side door, and it was that way that Dame Elizabeth came. They were still on their knees but Cecily sprang up at once, and ran to her.

'Your father is with me, child. Do you know yet what I was trying to tell you last night?'

'Yes,' said Cecily.

'Then all is well with you both; and with me. Good evening, Father. Shall we sing *Nunc Dimittis?*' She laughed a little. 'Sir Thomas and I have tired one another out with cursing and hatred. I think you need not fear him, Cecily.'

It was strange for Cecily to see her father there. Lewis

had her hand again, but for all that she trembled when
Sir Thomas entered. 'Sir,' she said, her voice shaking,
'I think you know this is Lewis Mallory, my husband.'

He stood in the half light by the altar steps and looked
her over slowly, head to toe and back again. He was tired
from the unending day, the pursuit and the fury, the
frustration of his plans and the triumph of his sister, whom
he could not love. He had grown his beard again and
perhaps there was some grey in it. It was possible to see
that he was no longer a man in the prime of life but one
whose disappointments, largely of his own making, had
taken their toll.

'This is my father, Lewis,' Cecily said, in the same
shaken tones.

'And shall I say: this is my daughter?'

'Indeed, sir—it is your daughter.' Looking at his
baffled, exhausted face, she felt her heart turn in her
breast with sorrow. For he had not always been harsh
with her. Her mother, it was said, had loved him at the
start. And between them there existed, whatever the
circumstances, the strange pull of shared blood.

'I could still take you back,' he said. 'You know that.
I could find a dozen ways of shaping you to my own will.
You know that—you know it still. It is not you who have
defied me, but my sister who has connived and plotted
to strike at me. Well—be comforted. She has succeeded.
If I took you back with me tonight, I swear I do not know
at all what I could do with you. Your aunt has made you
into a scarecrow.'

'They use the word *mawkin* hereabouts,' his sister said.

'And hereabouts is all she's fit for,' he said bitterly.
Again he looked at the torn and dirty gown, at her
tousled hair and roughened hands. Then his eye went
slowly and dismissively over Lewis. 'As he is.' He laughed,
then, but without any enjoyment. 'Well, my treasure, as I
once called you—you are well and truly spent. Your

fortune lies with your mother's brother, but you'll get a thin dowry from Lord Digby now. Ask your husband what he thinks of that?'

'Nothing, sir,' said Lewis. 'I know how to live, and that's what we need.'

'And besides,' said Dame Elizabeth, 'my rights in Mantlemass are confirmed in perpetuity. The one condition—I may not leave it in the female line. See that Lewis shares it with you, Cecily.'

'Shall we live there?' Cecily said. 'Is it possible? You have made Lewis your heir?'

'The will is drawn up, sealed by my sovereign—and so in every respect ratified.'

'God save my future from scheming women,' Sir Thomas said. Again he looked at his daughter. 'What a pretty thing you were that day—a rich relation to the wench you've become.' He heaved a great sigh. 'No blessings from me, child. But I am too tired for curses.'

He turned away and went slowly to the door and out of the chapel. They heard his horse stamp as he unhitched the bridle.

Cecily broke from Lewis and ran to the door. But he was already riding away. She called out, certain she would never see him again: 'Father . . . !'

She could just see through the darkness that he turned in the saddle briefly and raised his hand. How terrifying he had been in his power—how sad and lonely he seemed now in defeat. She still stood there, the last of her old life swallowed in the darkness. Then Lewis came out to her, putting his hand over the lark and the laurel slipping hugely on her finger.

'The smith could make it smaller,' he suggested. 'I cannot hope to hold it on your hand for ever!' He smiled. It was too dark for her to see, but she knew that he smiled. 'Come, wife,' he said. 'It's time we said our farewells and went home.'